SELMA LAGERLÖF (1858-1̶ Värmland, trained as a teacheɪ ɑɪɪu ɒᴇᴄɑɪɪɪᴇ, ɪɪɪ her life-time, Sweden's most widely translated author ever. Novels such as *Gösta Berlings saga* (1891; *Gösta Berling's Saga*) and *Jerusalem* (1901-02) helped regenerate Swedish literature, and the school textbook about Nils Holgersson who traverses Sweden on the back of a goose has become familiar the world over. Two very different trilogies, the Löwensköld trilogy (1925-28) and the Mårbacka trilogy (1920-32), the latter often taken to be autobiographical, give some idea of the range and power of Lagerlöf's writing. Several of her texts inspired innovative films, among them *Herr Arnes pengar* (*Sir Arne's Treasure*), directed by Mauritz Stiller (1919) and based on *Herr Arnes penningar* (1903; *Lord Arne's Silver*), and *Körkarlen* (*The Phantom Carriage*), directed by Victor Sjöström (1921) and based on Lagerlöf's *Körkarlen* (1912). She was awarded the Nobel Prize for Literature, as the first woman ever, in 1909, and elected to the Swedish Academy, again as the first woman, in 1914. Having been able to buy back the farm of Mårbacka, which her family had lost as the result of bankruptcy, Lagerlöf spent the last three decades of her life combining her writing with the responsibilities for running a sizeable estate. Her work has been translated into close to 50 languages.

On his retiral in 2009, **PETER GRAVES** was Head of the School of Literatures, Languages and Cultures at the University of Edinburgh, where he is now an Honorary Fellow in Scandinavian Studies. He has written extensively on Scandinavian literature and is also a translator, having translated works by Linnaeus, Jacob Wallenberg, August Strindberg and Peter Englund and others. He has been awarded a number of prizes and honours for his translation work.

Some other books from Norvik Press

Kjell Askildsen: *A Sudden Liberating Thought* (translated by Sverre Lyngstad)

Victoria Benedictsson: *Money* (translated by Sarah Death) (2011)

Hjalmar Bergman: *Memoirs of a Dead Man* (translated by Neil Smith)

Jens Bjørneboe: *Moment of Freedom* (translated by Esther Greenleaf Mürer)

Jens Bjørneboe: *Powderhouse* (translated by Esther Greenleaf Mürer)

Jens Bjørneboe: *The Silence* (translated by Esther Greenleaf Mürer)

Johan Borgen: *The Scapegoat* (translated by Elizabeth Rokkan)

Kerstin Ekman: *Witches' Rings* (translated by Linda Schenck)

Kerstin Ekman: *The Spring* (translated by Linda Schenck)

Kerstin Ekman: *The Angel House* (translated by Sarah Death)

Kerstin Ekman: *City of Light* (translated by Linda Schenck)

Arne Garborg: *Tha Making of Daniel Braut* (translated by Marie Wells)

P. C. Jersild: *A Living Soul* (translated by Rika Lesser)

Selma Lagerlöf: *Lord Arne's Silver* (translated by Sarah Death) (2011)

Selma Lagerlöf: *The Löwensköld Ring* (translated by Linda Schenck) (2011)

Viivi Luik: *The Beauty of History* (translated by Hildi Hawkins)

Henry Parland: *To Pieces* (translated by Dinah Cannell) (2011)

Amalie Skram: *Lucie* (translated by Katherine Hanson and Judith Messick)

Amalie and Erik Skram: *Caught in the Enchanter's Net: Selected Letters* (edited and translated by Janet Garton)

August Strindberg: *Tschandala* (translated by Peter Graves)

August Strindberg: *The Red Room* (translated by Peter Graves)

Hanne Marie Svendsen: *Under the Sun* (translated by Marina Allemano)

Hjalmar Söderberg: *Martin Birck's Youth* (translated by Tom Ellett)

Hjalmar Söderberg: *Selected Stories* (translated by Carl Lofmark)

Anton Tammsaare: *The Misadventures of the New Satan* (translated by Olga Shartze and Christopher Moseley)

Ellen Wägner: *Penwoman* (translated by Sarah Death)

THE PHANTOM CARRIAGE

by

Selma Lagerlöf

Translated from the Swedish
and with an Afterword
by Peter Graves

Series Preface by Helena Forsås-Scott

Norvik Press
2011

Originally published in Swedish by Bonniers Förlag under the title of
Körkarlen (1912)

This translation © Peter Graves 2011

This preface © Helena Forsås-Scott 2011

The translator's moral right to be identified as the translator of the
work has been asserted.

A catalogue record for this book is available from the British Library.

ISBN: 978-1-870041-91-1

Norvik Press gratefully acknowledges the generous support of The
Swedish Academy (Stockholm), The Swedish Arts Council (Stockholm),
The Anglo-Swedish Literary Foundation (London), and the Embassy of
Sweden (London) towards the publication of this translation.

Norvik Press
Department of Scandinavian Studies
University College London
Gower Street
London WC1E 6BT
United Kingdom

Website: www.norvikpress.com
E-mail address: norvik.press@ucl.ac.uk

Managing editors: Sarah Death, Helena Forsås-Scott, Janet Garton, C.
Claire Thomson.

Cover illustration: based on *Photograph of writer Selma Lagerlöf*, taken
in 1906 by A. Blomberg, Stockholm.

Layout: Elettra Carbone
Cover design: Sture Pallarp (winner of a competition run in cooperation
with Beckmans designhögskola in Stockholm and the Embassy of
Sweden in London).

Printed in the UK by Lightning Source UK Ltd.

Contents

Series Preface

In the first comprehensive biography of the Swedish author Selma Lagerlöf (1858-1940), Elin Wägner has provided a snapshot of her at the age of 75 that gives some idea of the range of her achievements and duties. Sitting at her desk in the library at Mårbacka with its collection of classics from Homer to Ibsen, Lagerlöf is also able to view several shelves of translations of her books. Behind her she has not only her own works and studies of herself but also a number of wooden trays into which her mail is sorted. And the trays have labels like 'Baltic Countries, Belgium, Holland, Denmark, Norway, England, France, Italy, Finland, Germany, Sweden, Switzerland, the Slavic Countries, Austria-Hungary, Bonnier [her Swedish publisher], Langen [her German publisher], Swedish Academy, the Press, Relatives and Friends, Treasures, Mårbacka Oatmeal, Miscellaneous Duties'. Lagerlöf's statement, made to her biographer Elin Wägner a few years previously, that she had at least contributed to attracting tourists to her native province of Värmland, was clearly made tongue in cheek.

How could Selma Lagerlöf, a woman born into a middle-class family in provincial Sweden around the middle of the nineteenth century, produce such an œuvre (sixteen novels, seven volumes of short stories) and achieve such status and fame in her lifetime?

Growing up on Mårbacka, a farm in the province of Värmland, at a time when the Swedish economy was predominantly agricultural, Selma Lagerlöf and her sisters learnt about the tasks necessary to keep the self-sufficient household ticking over, but their opportunities of getting an education beyond that which could be provided by their governess were close to non-existent. Selma Lagerlöf succeeded in borrowing money to spend three years in Stockholm training to become a teacher, one of the few professions open to women at the time, and after qualifying in 1885 she spent ten years teaching at a junior high school for girls in Landskrona, in the south of Sweden. Mårbacka had to be sold at auction in 1888, and Lagerlöf only resigned from her teaching post four years after the publication of her first novel, establishing herself as a writer in a Sweden quite different from the one in which she had grown up. Industrialisation in Sweden was late but swift, and Lagerlöf's texts found new readers among the urban working class.

Lagerlöf remained a prolific author well into the 1930s, publishing chiefly novels and short stories as well as a textbook for school children, and she soon also gained recognition in the form of honours and prizes: an Honorary Doctorate at the University of Uppsala in 1907, the Nobel Prize for Literature, as the first woman, in 1909, and election to the Swedish Academy, again as the first woman, in 1914. Suffrage for women was only introduced in Sweden in 1919, and Lagerlöf became a considerable asset to the campaign. She was also able to repurchase Mårbacka, including the farm land, and from 1910 onwards she combined her work as a writer with responsibility for a sizeable estate with a considerable number of employees.

To quote Lagerlöf's most recent biographer, Vivi Edström, she 'knew how to tell a story without ruining it'; but her innovative literary language with its close affinity with spoken language required hard work and much experimentation. 'We authors', Lagerlöf wrote in a letter in 1908, 'regard a book as close to completion once we have found the style in which it allows itself to be written'.

Her first novel, *Gösta Berlings saga* (1891; *Gösta Berling's Saga*), was indeed a long time in the making as Lagerlöf experimented with genres and styles before settling for an exuberant and innovative form of prose fiction that is richly intertextual and frequently addresses the reader. Set in

Värmland in the 1820s with the young and talented Gösta Berling as the hero, the narrative celebrates the parties, balls and romantic adventures throughout 'the year of the cavaliers' at the iron foundry of Ekeby. But it does so against the backdrop of the expulsion of the Major's Wife who has been benefactress of the cavaliers; and following her year-long pilgrimage and what has effectively been a year of misrule by the cavaliers, it is hard work and communal responsibility that emerge as the foundations of the future.

In *Drottningar i Kungahälla* (1899; *The Queens of Kungahälla*) Lagerlöf brought together a series of short stories and an epic poem set in Viking-age Kungälv, some distance north of Gothenburg, her aim being to explore some of the material covered by the medieval Icelandic author Snorri Sturluson in *Heimskringla*, but from the perspectives of the female characters. The terse narrative of *Herr Arnes penningar* (1903; *Lord Arne's Silver*), set in the sixteenth century in a context that reinforces boundary crossings and ambivalences, has a plot revolving around murder and robbery, ghosts, love and eventual punishment. The slightly earlier short novel *En herrgårdssägen* (1899; *The Tale of a Manor*) similarly transcends boundaries as it explores music and dreams, madness and sanity, death and life in the context of the emerging relationship between a young woman and man.

A few lines in a newspaper inspired Lagerlöf to her biggest literary project since *Gösta Berling's Saga*, the two-volume novel *Jerusalem* (1901-02), which also helped pave the way for her Nobel Prize later in the decade. The plot launches straight into the topic of emigration, prominent in Sweden since the 1860s, by exploring a farming community in the province of Dalarna and the emigration of part of the community to Jerusalem. The style was inspired by the medieval Icelandic sagas, but although the focus on emigration also established a thematic link with the sagas, the inversions of saga patterns such as bloody confrontations and family feuds become more prominent as the plot foregrounds peaceful achievements and international understanding. Yet this is first and foremost a narrative in which traditional structures of stability are torn apart, in which family relationships and relations between lovers are tried and often found wanting, and in which the eventual reconciliation between old and new comes at a considerable price.

Lagerlöf had been commissioned to write a school textbook in 1901, but it was several years before she hit on the idea of presenting the geography, economy, history and culture of the provinces of Sweden through the narrative about a young boy criss-crossing the country on the back of a goose. While working on *Nils Holgerssons underbara resa genom Sverige* (1906-07; *The Wonderful Adventures of Nils, Further Adventures of Nils*), Lagerlöf doubted that the text would find readers outside Sweden; paradoxically, however, *Nils Holgersson* was to become her greatest international success. Once perceived as an obstacle to the ambitions to award Lagerlöf the Nobel Prize for Literature, *Nils Holgersson* is nowadays read as a complex and innovative novel.

Körkarlen (1912; *The Phantom Carriage*) grew out of a request from The National Tuberculosis Society, and what was intended as a short story soon turned into a novel. The narrative about a victim of TB, whose death on New Year's Eve destines him to drive the death cart throughout the following year and who only gains the respite to atone for his failures and omissions thanks to the affection and love of others, became the basis in 1921 for one of the best-known Swedish films of the silent era, with Victor Sjöström as the director (Sjöström also played the central character) and with ground-breaking cinematography by J. Julius (Julius Jaenzon).

The First World War was a difficult time for Lagerlöf: while many of her readers, in Sweden and abroad, were expecting powerful statements against the war, she felt that the political events were draining her creative powers. *Kejsarn av Portugallien* (1914; *The Emperor of Portugallia*) is not just a novel about the miracle of a newborn child and a father's love of his daughter; it is also a text about a fantasy world emerging in response to extreme external pressures, and about the insights and support this seemingly mad world can generate. Jan, the central character, develops for himself an outsider position similar to that occupied by Sven Elversson in Lagerlöf's more emphatically pacifist novel *Bannlyst* (1918; *Banished*), a position that allows for both critical and innovative perspectives on society.

Quite different from Lagerlöf's war-time texts, the trilogy consisting of *Löwensköldska ringen* (1925; *The Löwensköld Ring*), *Charlotte Löwensköld* (1925) and *Anna Svärd* (1928) is at once lighthearted and serious, a narrative tour de force playing on ambivalences and multiple interpretations to an extent that has the potential to destabilise, in retrospect, any hard and fast readings of Lagerlöf's œuvre. As the trilogy calls into question the ghost of the old warrior General Löwensköld and then traces the demise of Karl-Artur Ekenstedt, a promising young minister in the State Lutheran Church, while giving prominence to a series of strong and independent female characters, the texts explore and celebrate the capacity and power of narrative.

Lagerlöf wrote another trilogy late in her career, and one that has commonly been regarded as autobiographical: *Mårbacka* (1922), *Ett barns memoarer* (1930; *Memories of My Childhood*), and *Dagbok för Selma Ottilia Lovisa Lagerlöf* (1932; *The Diary of Selma Lagerlöf*). All three are told in the first person; and with their tales about the Lagerlöfs, relatives, friends, local characters and the activities that structured life at Mårbacka in the 1860s and 70s, the first two volumes can certainly be read as evoking storytelling in the family circle by the fire in the evening. The third volume, *Diary*, was initially taken to be the authentic diary of a fourteen-year-old Selma Lagerlöf. Birgitta Holm's psychoanalytical study of Lagerlöf's work (1984) read the Mårbacka trilogy in innovative terms and singled out *Diary* as providing the keys to Lagerlöf's œuvre. Ulla-Britta Lagerroth has interpreted the trilogy as a gradual unmasking of patriarchy; but with 'Selma Lagerlöf' at its centre, this work can also be read as a wide-ranging and playful exploration of gender, writing and fame.

With the publication over the past couple of decades of three volumes of letters by Lagerlöf, to her friend Sophie Elkan (1994), to her mother (1998), and to her friend and assistant Valborg Olander (2006), our understanding of Lagerlöf has undoubtedly become more complex. While the focus of much of the early research on Lagerlöf's work was biographical, several Swedish studies centring on the texts were published in connection with the centenary of her birth in 1958. A new wave of Lagerlöf scholarship began to emerge in Sweden in the late 1990s, exploring areas such narrative, gender, genre, and aesthetics; and in the 1990s the translation, reception and impact of Lagerlöf's texts abroad became an increasingly important field, investigated by scholars in for example the US, the UK and Japan, as well as in Sweden. Current research is expanding into the interrelations between media in Lagerlöf, performance studies, and archival studies. As yet there is no scholarly edition of Lagerlöf, but thanks to the newly established Selma Lagerlöf Archive (Selma Lagerlöf-arkivet, SLA) a scholarly edition in digitised form is underway.

By the time Lagerlöf turned 80, in 1938, she was the most widely translated Swedish writer ever, and the total number of languages into which her work has been translated is now close to 50. However, most of the translations into English were made soon after the appearance of the original Swedish texts, and unlike the original texts, translations soon become dated. Moreover, as Peter Graves has concluded in a study of Lagerlöf in Britain, Lagerlöf 'was not well-served by her translators [into English]'. In other words, the publication of high-quality new translations into English of the major works of this Swedish author of world renown is long overdue.

Helena Forsås-Scott

Note
—Not the beginning of the story.

I

at the end of her life she
came to a place where her life
began

A poor little slum sister was dying. She had tuberculosis and within a year the end was near. She had carried on with her ordinary duties as long as she could and when her strength finally failed they sent her to a sanatorium. She was cared for there but did not improve, and realising there was no hope, she returned home to her mother who lived in a small house in a street on the edge of the town. Now she was confined to bed in the same small room she had occupied as a girl and was waiting to die.

Her mother sat at her bedside, anxious and grieving, so busy giving her daughter all the care she needed that she had no time for weeping. A slum sister who had worked with the sick woman stood at the foot of the bed and cried quietly, her eyes watching the dying woman's face with deep love. When tears came and misted her gaze, she wiped them away with a violent movement. A big woman with a large 'S' embroidered on the collar of her dress was sitting on a small uncomfortable chair which had been a particular favourite of the sick woman and been taken everywhere with her. They had offered her a different seat, but she had insisted on taking the uncomfortable chair as if as a mark of respect for the woman in the bed.

It was a day like any other, except that it was New Year's Eve. The sky was grey and heavy and to those who were sitting indoors it felt miserable and cold, although outside it was surprisingly mild. The ground was bare of snow and the one or two flakes that drifted gently down melted as soon as they touched the street. It looked as if there would soon be heavy snow, but it seemed reluctant to fall. It was as though wind and snow felt there was little point in causing more trouble during the old year, choosing rather to wait and save their strength for the arrival of the new.

Like the weather, the people seemed unable to make up their minds about what they should be doing. Nothing was happening outdoors and no work being done indoors. Right opposite the little house with the dying woman lay a plot where men had started driving in the piles for a building. That morning some workmen had arrived and, with the usual raucous work-songs, hauled up the massive pile-driver and let it drop. But after a short time they had wearied of it and gone away.

It was the same with everything else. Some women had hurried past with baskets to do their shopping for the holiday. That went on for a while but soon stopped. The children playing in the street had been called in to put on their holiday best, after which they had to stay indoors. Horses and carts drove past on their way to their stables out on the edge of town, where they would enjoy a full day's rest. Everything grew even quieter as the day drew on and it was a relief to hear the noises fading away one by one.

'It would be good if she could die on a day like today,' her mother said. 'Soon there will be no noise out there to disturb her.'

The sick woman had been unconscious since the morning. She could not have heard anything the three women said, but it was quite apparent that she was not lying in a dull torpor. Her face had changed several times during the morning, sometimes looking surprised and anxious, at other times pleading and, at others again, tormented. Now, however, for a long time, her expression had been one of concern – a concern so profound that it gave her face a look of exalted beauty.

The little slum sister's appearance had changed so much that her friend standing at the foot of the bed bent down to the other Salvationist and whispered:

'Captain, look! Sister Edit has become so beautiful she looks like a queen.'

The big woman rose from the low chair in order to see better.

Never before had she seen the little slum sister's face without the humble and happy expression it had worn, however sick and exhausted she may have felt. Now she was so amazed by the change that she remained standing.

With an impatient movement the sick woman had thrown herself up on her pillows so that she was sitting half upright in her bed. There was something indescribably sublime about her face, and although her mouth did not move, it looked as if her lips were ready to form chastening words.

Her mother looked up at the two surprised women.

'She has had that look on other days, too,' she said. 'Isn't this the time of day that she used to do her rounds?'

The slum sister cast a quick glance at the sick woman's battered watch that was ticking away on the bedside table. 'Yes,' she said, 'this is the time of day she used to visit the needy.'

Her voice broke off abruptly and she put her handkerchief to her eyes. Whenever she tried to speak she was unable to hold back the sobs.

The sick woman's mother took her daughter's small rough hand and stroked it. 'She has struggled too hard helping them keep their hovels clean and warning them against their vices,' she said in a voice that suggested repressed resentment. 'When your toils are too demanding, it is hard to put them out of mind. She imagines she is still doing her rounds among them.'

'That's how it can be when you love your duty so deeply,' the Salvationist captain said quietly.

They saw the sick woman's eyebrows draw together, the furrow between them growing deeper at the same time as her upper lip curled. They expected her eyes to open at any moment and flash with righteous anger.

'She has the look of an avenging angel,' the Salvationist captain said in a voice ringing with exultation.

'I wonder what they are doing down in the slums today?' said her companion, pushing past the others so that she could stroke the dying woman's brow. 'You must not worry about them now, Sister Edit. You have done enough for them.'

These words seemed to have the power to release the sick woman from the vision that was haunting her. The look of strain and exalted wrath that had marked her features slipped away and was replaced by the expression of quiet suffering she had worn throughout her illness.

She opened her eyes and when she saw her friend leaning over her she placed a hand on her arm and tried to draw her closer.

The slum sister did not understand the meaning of this light touch, but she recognised the pleading look in the sick woman's eyes and bent down close to her lips.

'David Holm,' the dying woman whispered.

Unsure whether she had heard properly, the slum sister shook her head.

The sick woman mustered all her strength in an effort to be understood. She repeated her words, pausing between each syllable.

'Send – for – Dav-id – Holm.'

She looked into her colleague's eyes until she was sure that her words had been understood. Then she lay back, and after a few minutes her thoughts had left them again and returned as before to some hateful scene that filled her soul with rage and torment.

The slum sister who had been leaning over the bed straightened up. She was no longer weeping. She was gripped by an emotion that had driven away the tears.

'She wants us to send for David Holm!'

The sick woman's request seemed truly dreadful and the Salvationist captain was as upset as her colleague.

'David Holm?' she repeated. 'That's impossible. We can't bring a man like David Holm to a dying woman!'

The sick woman's mother watched as her daughter's face once again took on the stern and wrathful expression of one demanding justice. She turned questioningly to the two flustered women.

'Sister Edit wants us to send for David Holm,' the captain said. 'But we don't know whether it is right to do so.'

'David Holm?' the sick woman's mother asked. 'Who is David Holm?'

'He is one of the people Sister Edit has been struggling with down in the slums. But the Lord has not given her any power over him.'

'Perhaps, captain,' the slum sister said hesitantly, 'it is God's intention to let her prevail over him now, in these her final hours?'

The sick woman's mother looked at her, reluctance showing in her eyes.

'You have had my daughter for as long as she had a spark of life. Let me have her for myself now that she is dying!'

That was the end of the matter. The slum sister returned to her place at the end of the bed. The Salvationist captain sat down again on the small chair, closed her eyes and quietly mumbled a prayer. The others could hear an occasional snatch of her prayer to God that the soul of the dying woman might depart this life in peace, untroubled by any further anxiety about the concerns of this world of tribulation.

She was deep in prayer when she was roused by the slum sister putting a hand on her shoulder. She opened her eyes quickly.

The sick woman had regained consciousness again, and again she had lost the mild and humble expression. As before, threatening storm-clouds were passing across her brow.

The slum sister quickly bent down to her and could hear the reproach in her voice.

'Sister Maria, why haven't you sent for David Holm?'

Her companion would have liked to voice her objections but there was something in the sick woman's eyes that silenced her.

'I shall bring him to you, Sister Edit,' she said. Turning to the dying woman's mother, she apologised, saying: 'I have never refused to do anything Sister Edit asked me and I cannot refuse her today'.

The sick woman closed her eyes with a sigh of relief and the slum sister left the little room. Everything fell silent once again. The captain, deeply anxious, prayed quietly, the dying woman's breathing became more laboured, and her mother moved closer to the bed as though to protect her poor child from suffering and death.

After a few seconds the sick woman opened her eyes again, with the same impatient expression. But when she saw that her colleague's place was empty, she understood that her request was being fulfilled and her face became milder. She made no effort to speak but she did not relapse into unconsciousness.

When the sound of the outside door opening was heard, she almost sat up in bed. The slum sister who had gone out appeared at the bedroom door, opening it little more than a crack.

'I won't come in,' she said, 'I'm much too cold. Captain Andersson, would you please come out here for a moment?'

The sick woman's eyes were fixed on her and she could see the look of expectation in them.

'I have been unable to find him,' she said. 'But I met Gustavsson and a couple of our people and they have promised me to seek him out. Gustavsson will bring him to you, Sister Edit, if it's at all possible.'

She had scarcely spoken these words before the dying woman closed her eyes and sank back into the inner contemplation that had filled her day.

'I think she is seeing him,' the slum sister said in a voice tinged with disapproval, but she quickly corrected herself: 'Hallelujah, it is the will of God and cannot be wrong.'

She withdrew quietly to the outer room and the captain followed her.

A woman was waiting there. She could have been little more than thirty years old but her skin was so grey and heavily lined, her hair so thin and her body so emaciated that life had been kinder to many much older women. Her clothes were so shabby she looked as if she had dressed in her worst rags ready to go out begging.

When the Salvationist captain looked at the woman she felt a surge of anxiety. Worse than her shabby clothing and premature signs of age was the frozen immobility of her features. This was a woman who moved and walked and stood but seemed to be ignorant of where she really was. She looked as if she had been through such appalling sufferings that her soul was clinging to the brink of an abyss of madness, into which it might plunge at any moment.

'This is David Holm's wife,' the slum sister said. 'I found her in this state when I went to their place to fetch him. He was out and she was alone there and utterly incapable of responding to anything I said to her. I didn't dare leave her so I brought her with me.'

'So this is David Holm's wife,' the captain said. 'I'm sure I've come across her somewhere before though I don't recognise her. What's wrong with her?'

'It's obvious what's wrong, isn't it?' the slum sister answered angrily, gripped by a sudden and impotent fury. 'It's her husband. He is tormenting her to death.'

The Salvationist captain looked at the woman hard and long. Her eyes were bulging in their sockets, pupils staring fixedly straight ahead. She was twisting and turning her fingers ceaselessly and a slight tremor repeatedly crossed her lips.

'What has he been doing to her?' she said.

'I don't know. She is unable to answer. She was sitting there trembling like this when I got there. The children were out and there was no one I could ask. Lord God, for this to happen today of all days. How can I take care of her when I only want to think of Sister Edit?'

'He must have been beating her.'

'Worse than that, I think. I've seen women who have been beaten and they aren't like this. No, this is something much worse,' she said with rising horror in her voice. 'We could see from Sister Edit's face that something dreadful must be going on.'

'Yes,' the captain exclaimed. 'Now we know what she was seeing! God be praised that Sister Edit saw it and you got there in time, Sister Maria. Thanks be to God! It is surely His will that we should save her sanity.'

'But what am I to do with her? She follows me when I take

her by the hand but she doesn't hear anything I say. Her mind has deserted her, and how are we to bring it back? I have no power over her. Perhaps you will have more success, Captain Andersson?'

The stout Salvationist captain took the poor woman's hand and spoke to her in a voice that was sometimes mild and sometimes stern, but the woman's face showed no sign of understanding.

While they were making these vain efforts, the sick woman's mother appeared at the door of the inner room.

'Edit is becoming anxious,' she said. 'I think you should come in to her.'

Both Salvationists hurried into the little bedroom, where they found the sick woman tossing and turning in her bed. Her restlessness seemed to be caused more by spiritual anxiety than by any physical pain. She grew calmer and closed her eyes as soon as she saw her two friends back in their usual places.

The captain gestured to the slum sister to stay with the sick woman while she herself rose to slip out again. But just then the door opened and David Holm's wife entered.

She went to the bed and stood there, staring with her empty eyes, trembling as before and twisting her rough fingers so violently that the joints cracked.

For a long time she gave no sign of knowing what she was looking at, but very slowly the fixed stare in her eyes began to soften. She bent forward, closer and closer to the face of the dying woman.

Then something strange and threatening seemed to come over the woman. Her twisted fingers separated and curved. The two Salvationists leapt up, afraid that she was about to hurl herself at the dying woman.

The dying slum sister opened her eyes, saw this dreadful, half-demented creature before her, sat up in bed and wrapped her arms around her. She drew the woman to her with all the strength she had left and kissed her face, her brow, her cheeks and her lips, whispering all the time, 'Oh, poor Mrs Holm! Poor Mrs Holm!'

At first the poor woman seemed to want to pull away, but suddenly a tremor ran through her body. She began to sob and sank down on her knees at the bedside, her head pressed to the dying woman's cheek.

'She is weeping, Sister Maria, she is weeping,' the captain whispered. 'She won't go mad.'

The Salvationist clutched her tear-sodden handkerchief tightly in her hand and, with a vain effort to keep her voice steady, she whispered:

'Sister Edit is the only one capable of that, captain, the only one. What are the rest of us to do when she is gone?'

Then they noticed the pleading look in the mother's eyes and the captain said: 'Come, we must take her out. It wouldn't be right, anyway, if her husband were to come and find her here.'

'No, Sister Maria, you stay with your friend,' the captain continued when she saw the slum sister rising to leave. 'I shall look after Mrs Holm.'

II

Later on this same New Year's Eve, when night had come and darkness fallen, three men were sitting drinking beer and schnapps in the small shrubbery that surrounds the parish church. They were sitting on a patch of withered grass under some lime trees, the black branches of which glistened with moisture. They had been in a bar earlier in the evening but when closing time came they moved out into the open air. They knew it was New Year's Eve, which was why they had chosen to sit in the church shrubbery: they wanted to be close enough to the clock tower to be sure of hearing midnight strike, marking the time to drink a toast to the New Year.

They were not sitting in darkness since the glow of the electric lamps in the surrounding streets lit up the bushes. Two of the men were old and decrepit – tramps who had slunk into town to spend the New Year drinking up what money they had managed to beg. The third was a man of a little over thirty. Like the other two, he was dressed in extremely shabby clothes, but he was tall and well-built and looked as if he was still healthy and strong.

Afraid of being discovered and moved on by the police, they were sitting close together so that they could talk quietly – whisper almost. The younger man was doing the talking and the other two were listening so attentively that it was some time since they had raised their bottles.

'I had a friend once,' the speaker said in an earnest, rather mysterious voice, although there was a malicious glint in his eye, 'who became a completely different man whenever it was New Year's Eve. Not because he had gone through his accounts and was dissatisfied with what he'd made in the year, but because he'd heard of something strange and dangerous that could happen to people on that particular day. I can assure you, gentlemen, that he would sit silent and anxious from morning till night without even looking at a drink. He wasn't usually given to being a misery, but on New Year's Eve there was less chance of him joining a little session of the kind we're having than there is of the Lord Lieutenant inviting you two in for a drink.

'Well, gentlemen, you'll be wondering what he was frightened of. It wasn't easy to get it out of him, but on one occasion he did tell me. Do you want me to tell you about it? Or perhaps not, since it might well be a bit creepy for you in this church shrubbery, which I imagine used to be a graveyard. What do you think, gentlemen?'

The two tramps were quick to assure him that ghosts held absolutely no fears for them. So he continued.

'The fellow I'm talking about was a better class sort of chap – he'd been a student at Uppsala and knew a bit more than the rest of us. And he made sure he stayed sober on New Year's Eve in order to avoid having an accident or getting involved in a fight, because he didn't want to risk dying on that day. Dying any other day didn't worry him, but New Year's Eve was different because he believed that if he died then he would be condemned to drive the death cart.'

'The death cart?' the two listeners repeated in a questioning tone.

The tall man took the opportunity to sharpen their curiosity by asking again whether they really wanted to hear a story like this in a place like this, but the two tramps urged him to continue.

'Well, this fellow claimed with absolute conviction that there is an ancient carriage – more of a cart, really, of the kind farmers use to take their produce to market – so dilapidated it isn't fit to be on the highway and so covered in mud and dirt you can hardly see what it's built of. The axle is broken, the iron hoops so loose that they rattle, and the Lord alone knows when the wheels were last greased since they screech and squeal enough to drive you mad. The floor is rotten, the driver's cushion is torn and half the seat back is broken and missing. The carriage is pulled by an old horse, one-eyed and lame and with its tail and mane grey with age. It's so skinny that its backbone sticks up through its skin like the teeth of a saw and you can count its ribs. Its legs are stiff and it is lazy and unwilling to move any faster than a child can crawl. The horse's harness is worn and moth-eaten, with all the hooks and buckles missing, so it's all tied together with bits of twine and withies. Not a single brass or silver boss left, just a few filthy tassels, which are more unsightly than decorative. The reins are in the same state as the harness, mended with knot after knot and completely beyond further repair.'

The speaker paused and reached for his bottle, mainly to give his listeners time to reflect on what they had heard.

'Now, gentlemen,' he resumed his story, 'you may think there is nothing very strange about this, but the fact is that, in spite of the wretched state of the harness and the reins, there is a driver sitting up there on the broken seat – a driver who is bent and hideous, his lips blue-black, his cheeks pallid and grey and his eyes as dull as tarnished mirrors. He is dressed in a filthy black cloak with a great hood that he pulls right down over his face, and in his hand he clasps the long shaft of a blunt and rusty scythe. The man with the knotted reins clutched in his hand is, of course, no ordinary driver, for he serves a stern master whose name is Death. His duty, day and night, is to drive round on his master's errands. If anyone is lying at death's door, the driver must go there as quickly as his creaking and rattling old cart and his lame horse can take him.'

The speaker paused once more and tried to catch a glimpse of his listeners' faces. When he saw that they were as attentive as he could possibly desire, he continued.

'I've no doubt, gentlemen, that you've seen portraits of Death and you'll probably recall that he is usually depicted on foot. But this is not Death himself, this is just his driver. A mighty lord like Death can only be expected to harvest the very finest crops, whereas the poor stragglers and weeds that grow by the roadside are gathered in by his driver. But, my friends, listen carefully now to the strangest part of my story: although it is always the same cart and always the same horse that make the rounds of the dying, it is not always the same driver. The last man to die in the year, the man who breathes his last breath as the clock strikes twelve on New Year's Night, is doomed to become Death's driver. His body will be buried just like any other corpse, but his ghost must don the cloak and grasp the scythe and travel from one house of death to another for a whole year. He has no hope of release until the following New Year.'

The speaker fell silent and looked at his two small companions, his eyes glinting with malicious expectation. He could see them staring up in a vain effort to see the hands of the church clock.

'The clock has just struck a quarter to twelve,' he informed them, 'so there is no doubt that the danger hour is upon us. Now, gentlemen, you will understand what my friend was afraid of – he was afraid he would die just as the clock struck twelve on New Year's Night and thus become the driver of the death cart. I believe he used to sit there the whole day imagining he could hear the rattle and creak of the cart and, do you know, the strange thing is that it seems he actually died last year on New Year's Eve.'

'Did he die just as the year was changing?'

'All I know is that he died on New Year's Eve. I don't know the exact time, but I could have predicted he would die on that day because he was so terrified by the thought. Were you two to believe what he believed, I shouldn't be surprised if the same thing happened to you.'

As if by common agreement, the two small men each grabbed a bottle by the neck and took a long swig. Then slowly and clumsily, they attempted to get to their feet.

'Come along gentlemen, you're not going to break up the party before the stroke of midnight, are you?' the narrator said when he saw how effectively he had frightened them. 'I can't believe you'd set much store by an old wife's tale like this. My friend, now, he was a soft sort of fellow, not sound old Swedish stock like us. Sit down and have another drink.'

'We may just as well stay here, anyway,' he said, once he had got them to sit down again. 'This is the first place I've been able to get any peace all day. Everywhere else I've shown my face I've been pestered by Sally Army people wanting me to go to Sister Edit. She's supposed to be dying. I've been ducking out of it – I can't be doing with their sickening sermonising.'

Befuddled by drink as they were, his two companions came to life at the mention of Sister Edit. They asked whether she was the woman who ran the slum refuge in town.

'Yes, she's the one,' the younger man answered. 'She's done me the honour of paying me special attention all year. I hope she isn't so dear to you two that you're going to let grief get the better of you.'

They must have had some memory of a good deed Sister Edit had done since they both declared with great determination that, in their opinion, if Sister Edit desired to see someone, that someone, whoever it may be, should go to her at once.

'I see, so that's what you two gentlemen think, is it,' said the younger man. 'Well, I'll go, but only if the two of you, who seem to know me so well, can tell me what joy there will be for Sister Edit in getting a visit from me.'

The two tramps did not bother to answer his question. They simply continued urging him to go, and when he still refused and quarrelled with them instead, they flew into a rage and announced they would give him a good beating unless he went of his own free will.

At this point they rose to their feet and rolled up their sleeves ready to set about him.

Their adversary, well aware that he was the biggest and strongest man in town, was suddenly seized by compassion for this pair of poor weaklings.

'If you really want to go through with this, gentlemen,' he said, 'then I'm ready for you whenever you like. But I have to say that we might as well settle it peacefully, particularly in view of what I've just been telling you.'

The two drunks had almost forgotten the cause of their annoyance, but now that their blood was up they hurled themselves at him with clenched fists. He was so sure of his superiority that he stayed sitting where he was, not even bothering to stand up. He just stretched out his arms and tossed his attackers aside as if they were a couple of pups. But, like pups, they kept coming back and one of them managed to land a really solid punch on his chest. A moment later the big man felt a warmth rising in his throat and filling his mouth and, knowing that one of his lungs was already shot, he realised he was starting to haemorrhage. He stopped fighting and threw himself to the ground as a gush of blood poured over his lips.

Bad as that was, the situation quickly took a turn for the worse because the two tramps, feeling his warm blood on their hands and seeing him sink to the ground, believed they had murdered him. They immediately took to their heels and left him there alone. Although the flow of blood soon stopped, it began again whenever he tried to get to his feet.

The night was not unduly cold but, lying there outstretched, he soon began to suffer from the damp and the chill and quickly recognised that his time was likely to be short unless someone came to his aid and took him into shelter. Since he was lying not far from the town centre, and since it was New Year's Eve, many people were still up and about. He could hear them in the streets round the church, though no one ventured into the shrubbery. They were so close he could hear the murmur of their voices and he found it hard to believe he was going to die for lack of help when help was so near.

He lay and waited for a while and the cold began to torment him more and more. At last, knowing that he was unable to rise to his feet, he decided to shout for help.

Fortune was not on his side, however, for just as he started calling the church clock in the tower above him began to strike twelve. The loud ringing drowned out his voice and his cries went unheard. Nor did he have a second chance, for the effort of shouting caused the bleeding to begin again, this time so violently that the sensation of all the blood being drained from his body quickly became a reality. 'It can't be true, it simply can't be true that I'm going to die as the clock strikes midnight,' he thought, and with that thought he sensed he was flickering out like a dying candle. As the last thunderous stroke of the clock died away and heralded the New Year, he sank into darkness and unconsciousness.

III

No sooner have the twelve resounding strokes of the church clock faded into the distance than a short, sharp creaking noise cuts through the air.

With just a moment's pause, the sound is repeated time after time as if emanating from the ungreased wheels of some sort of vehicle; but the sound is more piercing and more unpleasant than could be made by any ordinary carriage, however dilapidated. It signals anguish, it signals fear – fear of all the suffering and pain man can imagine.

It is fortunate, then, that the sound appears to be inaudible to most of those who have stayed up to welcome in the New Year. If they had heard it, if all these happy young people in the streets round the square and the shrubbery had heard it, their greetings of good cheer and a Happy New Year would have changed to lamentations at all the evil that lies in store for them and for their friends. If they had heard it, the little congregation keeping the New Year watch-night in the mission chapel would have heard the mocking shrieks and banshee calls of fallen spirits mingling with their New Year hymn of praise and thanks to God. If he had heard it, the speaker at the feast, standing with his champagne glass raised to toast the New Year, would have fallen silent and listened to the loathsome raven call, boding doom to all the hopes and desires he is raising. If they had heard it, all those keeping watch that night at home while quietly pondering on their deeds and utterances of the bygone year would have felt their souls torn by the cold talons of despair, and their hearts would have trembled in recognition of their own weakness and helplessness.

It is fortunate, then, that the sound of the creaking can be heard by one man alone, and he is a man who needs to be driven to self-contempt, distress and remorse. If that is possible.

IV

After the loss of so much blood, the man struggled to regain consciousness. He was aware that something was waking him, aware that a screaming bird – or whatever it may have been – was hovering above him and screaming shrilly as he lay unable to rouse himself.

Suddenly he was seized by the conviction that the sounds were not those of a bird but of the ancient death cart of the story he had told the tramps; it was approaching through the bushes, squealing and creaking and waking him. Then, lying half-conscious, he dismissed the thought as being no more than his imagination playing on thoughts that had been in his mind a short time before.

He sank back into a daze, but once again he heard the persistent squealing coming closer. It refused to leave him in peace and he began to wonder whether it was the creaking of a real carriage. Perhaps it was not his imagination after all, perhaps it was real – whichever it was, there seemed to be no hope of it ceasing.

He realised he must force himself to wake up. Nothing else would do.

He saw that he was lying in the same place and that no one had come to his aid. Everything was as before except for the short sharp creaks that were cutting the air. They seemed to be coming from far away, but they were so persistent and so piercing that he knew at once that these were the sounds that had woken him.

It seemed unlikely that he could have been unconscious for long since he could hear people close-by shouting 'Happy New

Year' to one another, which meant that it could not be too long past midnight.

The sounds continued and, having always been sensitive to screeching noises, he decided to stand up and move away to escape the noise. He could try, at least. Since regaining consciousness he had been feeling quite well, and the sensation of there being a great gaping wound in his chest had passed. He no longer felt cold and weary and, like a man in full health, he was no longer conscious of his body.

He was lying on his side, just as he had thrown himself down when the bleeding began, so the first thing to do was to turn over onto his back and test how much his weakened body could take. 'I'll push myself up on my elbow very, very carefully,' he thought, 'turn over and then lower myself again.'

He was accustomed, as we all are, to his body responding to whatever his mind commanded. Now, however, his body remained motionless and failed to obey the commands of his mind. It just lay there, utterly inert. He wondered whether he had been lying so long that he had frozen to ice. If he was frozen, that must surely mean he was dead, but he was alive, wasn't he, and could both see and hear? It wasn't that cold, anyway, since drips were falling from the trees above him.

He was so preoccupied with wondering what sort of strange paralysis had afflicted him that he had forgotten the distressing creaking sound for a while. Now he could hear it again. 'No point in hoping to escape that music, Holm,' he said to himself. 'You'll just have to put up with it as best you can.'

It was difficult to be patient and lie still when he had felt so healthy until a short time before, and he still did not feel ill. He made repeated efforts to crook his finger or at least to raise an eyelid but everything proved impossible. Thinking that he had somehow forgotten the knack of doing these things, he tried to work out how he had performed these actions before, when he could still move.

Meanwhile, however, the creaking sound continued to get nearer and was now close enough for him to hear that it was coming from some sort of carriage being driven very slowly along Långgatan towards the square. Given that the creak of the wheels was now accompanied by the rattle of decrepit coachwork and the skidding of a horse's hooves on the paving stones, it was obviously in a wretched condition. The dreadful death cart which his old friend found so terrifying could scarcely have sounded worse.

'You and me, Holm,' he thought, 'we don't usually have much time for the police, but if they were to turn up and put a stop to that din, we'd be grateful.'

Holm was given to boasting about his strength of mind, but he was now beginning to fear that the interminable creaking and rattling, along with everything else that had happened that night, would mark the end of that. The disagreeable thought occurred to him that he would be found lying where he was now, taken for dead, carried off wrapped in a shroud and buried. 'Then you'll have to lie there listening to everything that is said around your corpse. Which is not likely to be much more pleasant than the things you're hearing now.'

All at once, however, the sounds somehow led him to think of Sister Edit, not with any pangs of conscience, but with an angry feeling that she had somehow got the better of him.

The creaking filled the air and pierced his ears but failed to arouse any sort of remorse for the wrongs he had inflicted on others; it brought instead angry memories of the bad and disagreeable things others had done to him.

While he was thus bemoaning his lot, he paused and listened intently for a minute or so. The vehicle had driven the length of Långgatan without turning off towards the square. The horse was no longer skidding on the cobble-stones, its hooves were crunching on gravel and it was coming in his direction. It must have turned into the shrubbery round the church.

In his joy at the thought of rescue, Holm tried once more to rise to his feet and, as before, he failed. It was only his thoughts that were capable of movement.

But the fact that a carriage, however ancient, really was approaching made up for that, even if the creaking of its woodwork, the grating of its harness and the squeal of its ungreased wheels all sounded so utterly dilapidated that he began to fear it would fall to pieces before it reached him.

It was moving incredibly slowly and, lying there alone and helpless, he thought impatiently that it was taking longer to arrive than it really was. He could not for the life of him puzzle out what sort of conveyance would come driving into the church shrubbery in the middle of New Year's Night. The driver was likely to be drunk, given the route he was taking. In which case, he was not likely to be much help.

'It's the creaking that's really upsetting you, Holm,' he thought. 'But the carriage didn't turn off down another street as you expected it to, it's coming straight towards you.'

Whatever it was could be no more than a few yards away by now and its horrendous creaking was beginning to undermine his courage. It was becoming more than he could endure. 'Your luck's run out tonight, Holm,' he thought. 'It looks as if another bit of bad luck is approaching. This sounds like a real juggernaut and it's going to run over you and anything else in its path.'

A moment later he caught sight of it. What he saw was no juggernaut coming to crush him, but it was still enough to strike terror into his heart.

Unable to move his eyes or any other part of his body, Holm could only see what was straight in front of him. The creaking conveyance approached from one side and it moved into his field of vision bit by bit. The first thing to appear was the head of an ancient horse, with a grey forelock and blind in the eye that was turned to him. Then came the forequarters, with only a short stump left of one of its legs. The harness was patched together with pieces of twine and birch-withies and adorned with filthy tassels. Then the whole of the broken-down horse came into view, followed by a worn-out cart with a broken seat-back and loose, wobbling wheels: it was an ordinary farmer's cart for bringing produce to market, but in such an appalling condition that it looked incapable of carrying anything.

Up on the broken seat sat a driver whose appearance tallied exactly with the description David Holm had given the two tramps. He was clutching a set of reins that consisted of nothing but a row of knots, his hood was pulled down over his eyes and he was sitting bent and low, as if bowed by a weariness that no amount of sleep would ever remedy.

When Holm had passed out after the first severe haemorrhage, he had felt as if his soul was fluttering away like a dying flame. Not now, however: now he felt his soul shaken and twisted beyond any hope of recovery. Given all that had preceded the arrival of the cart, he might have expected to see something supernatural, but no such thought had crossed his mind. Now, when everything he had heard in the story appeared before his very eyes, he could not square it with anything he had ever experienced before.

'This business is driving you mad, Holm,' he thought, utterly bewildered. 'As if the destruction of your body wasn't enough, you are going out of your mind as well.'

What came to his rescue was the driver's face. The horse had stopped right in front of him and the driver straightened up, as if waking from a dream. With a weary movement he pushed back his hood and peered about him as though looking for something. Their eyes met and the man lying on the ground recognised an old acquaintance.

'Surely that's Georges,' he thought. 'He may be strangely dressed but I recognise him, I recognise him.'

'Where on earth can he have been all this time?' he continued, talking to himself. 'We haven't met all year. But, then, Georges is a free man, not tied by a wife and children like you, Holm. He's probably been away on a long trip – to the North Pole, even. He certainly looks pale and frozen.'

He looked closely at the driver, thinking there was something strange about his expression. But it must be Georges, his old friend and drinking companion, it must be. He could recognize him by his large head and his aquiline nose, by the enormous black moustache and the Vandyke beard. A man like that, with the appearance any sergeant-major, indeed, any general, would be proud of, could not fail to be recognized by an old friend.

37

'But it can't be him, can it?' Holm continued talking to himself. 'You were told that Georges died in hospital in Stockholm last New Year's Eve, weren't you? But it wouldn't be the first time that we have got things wrong. But there's no doubt that this is Georges – just look at him when he stands up. Couldn't be anyone but Georges, with that delicate body so out of proportion to the soldierly head. When he jumped down from the cart and his cloak flew open, you could see he was still wearing that long, ragged coat which always hung down to his heels? Still buttoned right up to the neck, as always. Still the same big red neckerchief flapping round his throat. No sign of a waistcoat or shirt. All just as it used to be.'

Paralysed as he was, Holm felt his spirits revive. If it had been possible for him to laugh, he would have burst out laughing.

'Once we have got our strength back, Holm, we'll make Georges pay for this prank. All his dressing-up and play-acting have come close to driving us demented. Only Georges could have come up with the idea of driving up to the church in a horse and cart as wretched as that. Admit it, Holm, even you couldn't have come up with a scheme of that sort. Georges has always been more than a match for you.'

The driver walked over to where Holm lay and looked down at him. His face was set and earnest. It was obvious that he had no idea who the man on the ground was.

'There are several things I can't work out in all this business,' Holm thought. 'One is how he found out that I'd be sitting here on the grass with my companions so he could come and give us a fright. The other is how he could bring himself to dress up as the driver of the death cart he has always been so afraid of.'

Still showing no sign of recognition, the driver bent down over Holm.

'This poor wretch is not going to be too happy when he discovers that he has to take over from me,' Holm heard the driver mutter to himself.

Leaning on his scythe, the driver bent down closer and all at once he recognized his friend. He bent right down to him, impatiently threw back his hood and looked him in the eye.

'Oh!' he exclaimed. 'It's David Holm! The one person I thought would not be getting a visit from me! Oh, David, what a pity that it's you, what a pity!' he said, throwing his scythe to the ground and kneeling by the prostrate man.

When he spoke again, his voice rang with sincerity and sorrow. 'For the whole of this year I have longed for the chance to say just one word to you before it was too late. I came close to doing so once but you resisted and I couldn't get through to you. I thought I'd have a chance to do it the moment I was released from my duties, but now you're already lying here and it's too late for me to come and warn you to be on your guard.'

Holm listened to these words in complete confusion.

'What does he mean?' he thought. 'He is talking as if he were dead. When did he come close to me but I resisted him?' Then Holm calmed down: 'Of course! He has to talk like that! He has to act the part he's playing!'

'Believe me, David,' the driver continued in a voice trembling with emotion, 'believe me, I know it's my fault that you've been brought so low. If you hadn't met me you'd have been living a quiet and decent life. You and your wife would have worked your way up in the world. You were young and capable, both of you, and nothing would have held you back. Not a day has passed during this endless year, David, without me grieving over the way I lured you away from your life of diligence and industry and taught you my own evil ways. Oh the pity of it!'

The driver passed his hand over Holm's face before continuing: 'I fear you have strayed farther than I could ever have imagined. The course of your life can be traced in these terrible marks around your eyes and your mouth.'

Holm's good spirits were beginning to give way to impatience. 'The joke has gone far enough now, Georges,' he thought. 'Go and find someone to help lift me up on your cart and get me to hospital as quickly as you can.'

'You must know what my task has been for the last year,' the driver said. 'You must know the nature of the cart that brought me here, and I hardly need tell you who is to take over the scythe and hold the reins now that my time is done. But remember this, David: I am not the one who decided that this should be your fate. During the awful year that lies ahead of you, don't imagine for one moment that I could have avoided coming for you tonight. If there had been a choice, I'd have done anything to prevent you having to endure what I have endured.'

'Perhaps it's actually Georges who has gone mad?' David Holm thought. 'Otherwise he'd see that it's a matter of life or death for me and we can't just waste time like this.'

While Holm was thinking these thoughts, the driver looked at him with an expression of great sadness.

'There is no need to worry about getting to hospital, David. Once I come to a sickbed, it is too late to call any other doctor.'

'Every devil and demon must be out tonight and determined to cause trouble,' Holm thought. 'Someone turns up at last and could help me, but then he turns out to be either so mad or so malevolent he doesn't even enquire how badly injured I am.'

'Let me remind you of something that happened last summer, David,' the driver said. 'It was a Sunday afternoon and you were walking along the high-road through a broad valley with great fields and beautiful farms and blooming gardens on all sides. It was one of those sweltering afternoons we sometimes have in high summer and you realised you were the only one moving in the whole district. Even the cows in the meadows were standing still, afraid to venture out of the shade of the trees. There was not a human being in sight – everyone had gone indoors to avoid the heat. Do you remember, David, do you remember?'

'It's quite possible,' Holm thought. 'I've been out on the road in all weathers so often that I can't remember it all.'

'When everything was as silent and still as could possibly be, David, you heard creaking noises behind you on the road and thought there was someone driving along, though you couldn't see anyone. You looked round several times and thought it was one of the most peculiar things you had ever experienced. You could hear the creaking quite clearly but where was it coming from? It was broad daylight, open on every side, and the silence was so intense there was nothing else to confuse the sound. You simply couldn't understand how it was possible to be hearing the creak of wheels and yet be unable to see any sign of a vehicle. Of course, you refused to entertain the thought that there might be something supernatural about it – if you had been able to accept that possibility, I could have revealed myself to you before it was too late.'

Distinct memories of that day began to come back to Holm. He remembered looking behind fences and peering into ditches in an attempt to discover what was following him. He had eventually been frightened enough to go into a farm to escape the noise. When he came out again, everything was silent.

'That was the only time I've seen you this year,' the driver continued. 'I did everything I could to make you see me, but it wasn't in my power to come any closer. You could hear the creaking, but you walked along beside me like a blind man.'

'I can certainly remember the creaking,' Holm thought. 'But what is he trying to prove? That he was the one driving along the road beside me? I suppose I may have told the story to someone and they passed it on to Georges.'

The driver bent over Holm and spoke in the voice of someone rebuking a sick child: 'It's no good fighting it, David. You can't be expected to understand what has happened to you, but you know only too well that I, even though I'm speaking to you, am not a living man. You've been told that I'm dead, but you are refusing to accept it. And even if you hadn't been told, you have seen me driving this cart. No one who is still alive is ever carried in this cart, David.'

He pointed at the ramshackle cart that was standing in the middle of the gravel walk. 'Don't just look at the cart, David, look at the trees behind it.'

David Holm did as he said and for the first time he had to admit he was in the presence of something he could not explain. He could see the trees on the far side of the walk – he could see them right through the ancient cart.

'You've heard my voice many times in the past,' the driver

41

said. 'You can't fail to have noticed how differently I speak now.'

Holm was forced to agree. Georges had always had a beautiful voice, as did the driver, but it was quite a different sort of voice. Its tone was now thin and tinkling and it was difficult to hear; the same musician was playing, but the instrument itself was different.

The driver stretched out his hand and Holm saw how a small, clear drop of water fell from the wet branches above and passed right through the driver's hand before splashing onto the ground beneath.

A small twig lay on the gravel walk in front of them. The driver took his scythe, slid it underneath and raised it through the twig. The twig remained where it was, intact and uncut.

'Do not misunderstand me, David,' the driver said. 'Try to understand. You can see me and you think that I am as I was before. But this body of mine is only visible to those who are dead or lying on their deathbed. That does not mean it is a nothing – it is still home to my soul, just as your body is to yours. But don't think of it as being solid or heavy or strong, think of it as being like an image you see in a mirror; try to imagine that the image has stepped out of the glass and can see and speak and move.'

Holm's mind no longer tried to resist. He looked truth in the eye, no longer attempting to avoid it. The ghost of a dead man was talking to him and his own body was that of a dead man. But while conceding this, he felt a terrible rage growing within him. 'I will not be dead,' he thought. 'I will not be a nothing, not be a mere phantom. I want a fist I can strike with, a mouth I can eat with.' His rage gathered into a dense, black cloud, choking and loathsome, as yet tormenting no one but himself, but ready to explode at the first opportunity.

'There is something I would like to ask you, David, since you and I were good friends in the old days,' the driver said. 'You know as well as I do that there comes a time when the body is so worn and weary that the soul that inhabits it must leave. But the soul trembles and shakes with fear at having to enter an unknown country. It stands there rather like a small child on the seashore, frightened to step into the waves. To help it take the plunge the soul must hear the voice of someone who has gone before, someone already in the infinite, who can make it understand that there is no danger in taking that step. I have been such a voice, David, for a whole year, and now you must be that voice for the year to come. What I ask of you is that you do not resist your fate. Accept it humbly or you will bring great suffering to yourself and to me.'

Having spoken, the driver bent his head to look into David Holm's eyes. The resistance and defiance he saw there was enough to fill him with fear.

'You must understand, David,' he said in tones even more urgent than before, 'that this is not something you can escape. My knowledge of things on the other side is still slight. I have only travelled on its borders, so to speak, but I have seen enough to know that no mercy is given. Whether you choose to do so with good will or with ill, you will have to fulfil whatever duty is laid upon you.'

Once again he looked into David Holm's eyes and met nothing but a great dark cloud of anger.

'I will not deny,' he went on, 'that sitting on this seat and driving this horse from door to door is the most dreadful task anyone can be given. Wherever you come you will meet nothing but tears and lamentation, you will see nothing but disease and destruction, wounds, blood and horror. Yet that is perhaps the least terrible part. Worse to behold is what lies within – the agony, the remorse and the terror at what might lie in store. I have told you that the driver is only standing at the threshold. He thinks as men think; he only sees injustice and disappointment and unfairness and failure and disorder. He cannot see far enough into the other world to discern a purpose and a guiding hand. He may sometimes catch a glimpse of it, but mostly he must struggle on in darkness and in doubt. It may only be for one year that the driver is doomed to drive the death cart, but his time is not measured in earthly hours and minutes, it is extended to allow him to reach all the places he needs to reach; thus the single year can be as long as hundreds and thousands of mortal years. And there is more: although the driver knows that he is only doing what he has been commanded to do, it is impossible to describe the disgust and loathing he feels for himself, his sense of being a pariah because of his office. But worse, far worse than all that, David, is that in the course of his journeys the driver will meet the consequences of the evil he himself has committed during his life on earth – that is his inescapable fate ...'

At this, the pitch of the driver's voice rose almost to a scream and he wrung his hands in anguish, but a moment later he perceived once more the icy flood of scorn from his old friend, and he drew his cloak around him as though feeling its chill.

'David,' he continued insistently, 'however difficult the task may be, you must not fight against it – not unless you want to make things even worse for the two of us than they already are. I am not permitted to leave you alone: my task is to teach you to carry out your duties and I fear that may be the heaviest burden ever placed upon my shoulders. You can resist my efforts as long as you wish. You can keep me bound to the scythe for weeks and months, until next New Year even. My year may have expired, but I shall not gain my freedom until I have taught you to fulfil your duties with good will.'

While the driver was speaking, he had been on his knees in front of David Holm and his words were given more force by the sincerity with which they were uttered. He remained on his knees a moment longer, searching for any sign that his words had had an effect. But it was clear that his former friend was determined to resist to the last. 'I may be dead,' Holm was thinking, 'and I can do nothing to change that, but nothing, nothing, will induce me to have anything to do with this death cart and death horse. They will have to find some other task for me, because I will have nothing to do with this one.'

Before rising to his feet, the driver continued.

'Bear this in mind, David, that up to now it has been Georges speaking to you! From now on it is Death's driver you will have to deal with. You would do well to remember who people mean when they speak of the One by whom no man is spared.'

The next moment the driver rose to his feet with his scythe in his hand and his hood drawn down over his brow.

'Prisoner, come forth from your prison!' he called in a loud and ringing voice.

Instantly David Holm rose from the ground. He did not know how it happened but suddenly he found himself standing upright. He was swaying, and the church wall, the trees and everything around him seemed to be spinning.

'Look round, David Holm!' a forceful voice commanded, and after a moment's confusion he obeyed. Lying outstretched on the ground before him was a tall, powerfully built man in filthy rags. The man lay there, spattered with blood and soil, surrounded by empty bottles, his swollen face so red and blotchy that it was impossible to discern its original features. A stray beam of light from the distant streetlamps was reflected as a malevolent gleam of hatred in his narrowed eyes.

Holm stood there in front of this prostrate figure and saw that he was the dead man's double.

And yet he was not a double, for he was a nothing. Or it is wrong, perhaps, to say he was a nothing, he was an image, rather. An image of the dead man as seen in a mirror, an image that has stepped out of the glass and lives and moves.

Holm turned round quickly and saw Georges, and he saw now that Georges too was nothing, he too was an image of the body he had once occupied.

'O thou soul, that lost dominion over thy body at the instant of the New Year's striking,' Georges said, 'thou shalt deliver me from my duties. Thou shalt free souls from their earthly travails for the year to come.'

At these words David Holm became his old self. In a storm of rage he hurled himself at the driver, snatching at his scythe to shatter it and grasping at his cloak to tear it.

But he felt his hands being forced down and his legs pulled from under him; he sensed invisible bonds binding his wrists and his ankles. Then he was lifted and, like a dead thing, flung roughly onto the bottom of the cart.

A moment later the cart set off.

V

The room, though long and narrow, was quite large. It was in a house on the edge of town, a house so small that this one room took up almost all the space apart from one much smaller room used as a bedroom. In the light cast by a lamp hanging from the ceiling, the room looked homely and welcoming – rather more than that, in fact, it was the kind of happy room that could bring a smile to the face of anyone who entered. It was immediately obvious that whoever lived there had taken the trouble to arrange things to look like a proper home. The entrance was in one of the gable ends and there was a small stove right beside the door. That was the kitchen, and all the necessary kitchen fittings were there. The middle of the room was furnished as a dining room, with a round dining table, a couple of oak chairs, a tall wall clock and a small cupboard for glass and china. The lamp hung down above the table but it gave enough light to reach the innermost part of the room – the parlour – which was furnished with a mahogany sofa, an occasional table, an Axminster rug with a flower pattern, a palm in a splendid china pot and many photographs.

The arrangement of the furniture had always been a source of humour when visitors came. When a good friend came in from the street, it was fun to lead him through to the parlour and then apologise for leaving him alone there since there was work to be done in the kitchen. At the dining table, which stood so close to the kitchen that you could still feel the heat from the stove, the joke was to say with great pomposity: 'Ring for the housemaid to come and take away the plates!' If the children started crying in the kitchen, their tears could be turned to laughter by joking with them that their cries were so loud they would disturb their father, who was sitting in one of the inner rooms.

Such were the thoughts the room normally evoked, but gentle and bright thoughts were not in the minds of the two men who entered shortly after midnight that New Year's Night. Both of them were so ragged and down-at-heel that they could have been taken for ordinary tramps had it not been that one of them was wearing a black cloak over his rags and carrying a long rusty scythe in his hand. It was scarcely the usual dress for a tramp and, stranger still, was the way he had entered the room without unlocking the lock or even opening the door – he had simply passed through it, locked and bolted as it was. The second man did not have the same terrifying symbols as the first, but there was something about him that made him even more frightening than his companion. His hands and feet were tied and he was being carried and dragged by the other man, who then hurled him contemptuously to the floor, where he lay like a filthy heap of rags and misery. The wild rage that flamed in his eyes and distorted his face inspired dread.

The room was not empty when the two men entered. Sitting at the table in the dining room they saw a young man with gentle features and a beautiful, childlike expression and, opposite him, a small and delicate woman who was just a little older. The man was wearing a red jacket with the words Salvation Army embroidered across the chest in bold letters. The woman wore a black dress without any obvious insignia, but on the table in front of her lay a bonnet of the kind usually worn by the slum sisters: she, too, was a Salvationist.

Both of them were deeply distressed. The woman was weeping silently and drying her eyes time and again with a wet and crumpled handkerchief. She did so impatiently, as if the tears were preventing her doing things she ought to have been doing. The man's eyes were also red with weeping but he would not allow his grief to get the better of him in front of her.

Now and then they said a few words to one another and it was obvious from their words that their thoughts were elsewhere, in the inner room with a sick woman, whom they had left so that her mother could be alone with her for a while. However preoccupied with the sick woman they were, it was strange that neither of them noticed the two men. The latter, of course, remained silent and still, one of them standing upright and leaning on the doorpost, the other lying crumpled at his feet. But the arrival of these visitors through locked doors in the dead of night might have been expected to shock the two Salvationists at the table.

The man lying on the floor, anyway, was surprised to see them looking towards him and his companion time after time without appearing to be aware of their presence. He could see everything. As he and Georges had travelled across the town, everything had seemed to him as before, as if he had been seeing it with ordinary mortal eyes – yet no one could see him. In his fury, the man had been hoping to terrify his enemies by revealing himself as he now was, but he had come to understand that he could not make himself visible to them.

He had never been in this room before, but since he knew the two people sitting at the table, he had no doubt where he was. If there was anything more calculated to increase his anger, it was this, to have been dragged against his will to a place he had spent yesterday refusing to visit.

Suddenly the Salvation Army soldier at the table pushed his chair back.

'It's past midnight,' he said. 'Holm's wife thought he would come home about this time. I'll go and try once more to get him to come.'

He stood up slowly and reluctantly and began to put on his coat, which had been hanging on the back of his chair.

'I can understand why you don't think there is any point in fetching him, Gustavsson,' the young woman said, struggling hard to hold back her tears. 'But remember, it's the last request Sister Edit will make of you.'

The soldier hesitated as he was putting his arm into the sleeve of his coat.

'Sister Maria,' he said, 'it may be the last service I can peform for Sister Edit but I still hope that David Holm won't be at home or will refuse to come with me. I've talked to him several times today, just as you and Captain Andersson commanded, and I've been glad that neither I nor anyone else has succeeded in making him agree to come.'

The prostrate figure on the floor gave a start when he heard the mention of his name, and an ugly sneer spread across his face.

'That fellow seems to have a bit more sense than the rest of them,' he muttered.

The slum sister looked up at the soldier and spoke quite sharply, her voice cutting through her tears: 'This time it would be good if you put things to Holm in such a way that he realises that he has to come.'

The soldier walked towards the door with the look of a man who is obeying a command but remains unconvinced. 'Should I bring him even if he is dead drunk?' he asked from the door.

'Gustavsson, just bring him, I would go so far as to say dead or alive. If the worst comes to the worst, he can lie here and sleep it off. The important thing is to get hold of him.'

The Salvationist's hand was already on the latch when he suddenly turned round and walked back to the table.

'I don't think a man like David Holm should come here,' he said, the colour draining from his face. 'Sister Maria, you know as well as I do the kind of man he is. Do you really think it's the right thing to do? Do you really think it's right to bring a man like that here?' the soldier said, pointing to the door of the small bedroom.

'If I thought ...' she began, but he would not let her finish.

'You know, don't you, Sister Maria, that if he comes it will only be to mock us? He will go round boasting that one of the slum sisters was so much in love with him that she couldn't even die without seeing him.'

The slum sister looked up quickly and a sharp retort was on her lips but she bit it back.

'I can't bear the thought of him talking about her! Least of all when she is dead,' the soldier exclaimed.

The slum sister's answer was solemn and emphatic. 'And are you so sure, Gustavsson, that David Holm would be wrong if he did say that?'

The bound figure lying on the floor by the door felt a sudden rush of joy and astonishment on hearing these words. He looked up to see whether Georges had noticed his reaction. The driver was still standing motionless but, to make sure he understood, Holm mumbled that it was a pity he had not known this while he was still alive – it would have been something to boast to his mates about.

The soldier was so shocked by Sister Maria's words that he felt the walls of the room spinning around him and he gripped the back of the chair.

'How can you say such a thing, Sister Maria? Surely you don't expect me to believe that ...?'

The slum sister's response was vehement. She squeezed her handkerchief tightly in her fingers and her words poured out in a torrent, as if she was hurrying to voice them before caution returned and stopped her.

'Who else would she hold so dear? You and me, Gustavsson, and everyone else who came to know her, allowed her to captivate and convert us. We couldn't resist her. We didn't laugh at her or mock her. There is no reason for her to feel anguish or remorse for our sakes. Neither you nor I, Gustavsson, are responsible for her lying where she is now lying.'

This outburst seemed to calm the soldier down.

'I didn't realise you were talking about loving sinners, Sister.'

'Nor am I, Gustavsson.'

This firm assurance gave one of the ghosts an immediate sense of elation. He attempted to smother it, afraid it might dispel his rage and desire to resist. He had been taken by surprise, having expected to be met with nothing but preaching. He resolved to be on his guard in future.

Sister Maria sat and bit her lip to control her emotions. Suddenly, however, she came to a decision.

'It won't do any harm to talk to you about it now, Gustavsson,' she said. 'Nothing matters now she is dying. Sit down and I'll explain things.'

The soldier took off his coat again and returned to his seat at the table. Without saying a word he sat down, his faithful eyes fixed expectantly on the slum sister.

'Let me first tell you how Sister Edit and I spent New Year's Night last year,' she said. 'During the autumn, headquarters decided to open a slum refuge in this town and the two of us were sent to set it up. There was a fearful amount of work to do but the Brothers and Sisters did everything in their power to help us and by New Year's Eve we had reached the point when we could move in. The kitchen and the dormitories were ready and we hoped to be able to open the refuge on New Year's Day itself, but we had to delay because the sterilising oven and the wash-house weren't ready.'

At the start of her account the slum sister found it hard to hold back her tears, but as the story progressed and she could move away from the present situation, her voice became firmer.

'You weren't in the Army at that stage, Gustavsson, otherwise you would have been with us on that joyful New Year's Eve. Some of the Brothers and Sisters came to visit us and we were able to offer them tea in our new home. You can't imagine how happy Sister Edit was to have been able to open a slum refuge in her home town where she knew all the poor and what they needed. She took such pleasure in walking around looking at the blankets and the mattresses and our newly-painted walls and our gleaming cooking pots that we couldn't help laughing at her. Happy as a sand-boy, as the saying goes. And you know, don't you, Gustavsson, that when Sister Edit was happy, all of us were happy.'

'Hallelujah!' the Salvationist soldier said. 'I know that.'

'The joy lasted as long as our friends were with us, but as soon as they had gone she was overwhelmed by anguish at all the evil in the world and she asked me to pray with her that we would not be defeated by it. We went down on our knees and prayed for our refuge and for ourselves and for all those we hoped to succour in their distress. As we knelt in prayer, the bell at the front door rang.

'Our friends had just left, so we thought that one of them must have forgotten something and come back to fetch it. But for safety's sake we both went to the door. When we opened up, it wasn't our friends but one of the people the refuge had been set up for.

'I can tell you, Gustavsson, that when I saw him in the doorway, big and ragged and drunk, he looked so dreadful that I was terrified and was tempted to make an excuse that the refuge wasn't open yet and so he'd have to go away. But Sister Edit was happy that God had sent her a guest. She thought God was showing us that He looked upon our work with favour. She brought him in and offered him supper, but he swore at her and said he just wanted to lie down. We took him into a dormitory and he just pulled off his coat, threw himself down on a bunk and the next moment he was asleep.'

'Imagine her being afraid of me!' Holm said to himself, but not without hoping that the motionless figure behind him would hear that he was the same old David Holm as before. 'What a shame that you can't see me the way I look now. I bet that would frighten the life out of you!'

'Sister Edit was keen to show special kindness to the first person to come to our refuge,' the slum sister continued, 'and I could see she was disappointed when he just fell asleep. But a moment later, when she caught sight of the state of his coat, she was happy again. I don't think I've ever seen anything so dirty and ragged. It gave off such a stench of filth and drink that it was hard to go near it. When I saw Sister Edit go over and start inspecting it, I was filled with dread and told her to leave it where it was since, without the oven and the wash-house, we had no way of disinfecting it.

'For Sister Edit, however, it was as if this man had been sent by God, and it was a joy for her to have the chance to mend his clothes. I couldn't stop her, Gustavsson, nor would she allow me to help. She told me I'd said the coat might be infected, so it wouldn't be right for me to handle it. As I was her subordinate, she was responsible for me and it was her job to see that I didn't do anything that might endanger my health. Then she sat down and stitched away at that coat for the whole of New Year's Eve.'

The Salvationist soldier sitting at the other side of the table raised his hands and clapped them together ecstatically: 'Hallelujah! Let us praise and give thanks to Almighty God for Sister Edit!'

'Amen, amen!' the slum sister said, joining him in jubilation. 'Let us thank and praise the Lord for Sister Edit! Let us thank Him that she was as she was, that she would spend the whole night sewing that filthy coat as joyfully as if it had been a king's mantle.'

A strange sense of rest and repose came over the man who had been David Holm when he thought of the young woman sitting in the peace of night mending a poor tramp's coat. After everything that had angered him, there was something healing and calming about that scene. If Georges had not been standing over him, dark and unmoving but watching his every movement, he would have liked to dwell on it for longer.

The slum sister took up her story again. 'God be praised that Sister Edit has never regretted sitting there until four o'clock in the morning sewing on buttons and putting on patches without giving a thought to the infection she was breathing. God be thanked that she has never regretted sitting in a room where the bitter cold of the winter's night seeped into her bones before she let herself go to bed.'

'Amen, amen!' said the Salvationist soldier.

'She was chilled through before she was finished,' the slum sister said. 'I could hear her twisting and turning for hours, unable to get warm. Scarcely had she gone to sleep before it was time to rise, but I did manage to convince her to stay in bed and let me take care of the guest, should he wake before she was fully slept.'

'You have always been a good friend to her, Sister Maria,' the soldier said.

'I know what an act of self-denial that was for her,' the slum sister continued with a slight smile, 'but she did it for my sake.

53

And she wasn't allowed to lie in for long, anyway, because as the man was drinking his coffee he asked if it was me who had mended his coat. When I said no, he asked me to fetch the sister who had helped him in that way.

'He was quiet and sober by then, and his way with words was better than you expect from men of that kind. Since I knew it would mean a great deal to Sister Edit to hear his words of thanks, I went and fetched her. She did not look like someone who had been up most of the night. There was a delicate pink flush on her cheeks and the look of joyful anticipation on her face made her so pretty that the man was quite taken aback at the sight of her. He had been standing in the doorway with such a vicious expression on his face that I was afraid he was intending to attack her, but his face brightened when he saw her. 'There's no danger now,' I thought. 'He won't do anything to her. No one would ever want to hurt her.'

'Hallelujah, hallelujah!' the soldier agreed.

'But then his face darkened again, and when she went up to him he pulled open his coat so violently that the new buttons were torn off. Then he shoved his hands down so hard into the pockets she had mended that we could hear them tearing, after which he ripped the lining of the coat so that it was even more ragged than when he had arrived. "You see, Miss," he said, "this is the way I like it to be! This is the way it's most comfortable! Pity you went to so much trouble – not that I can help it!"'

The ghostly figure lying on the floor recalled the sudden clouding of a woman's face which a moment before had been shining with happiness. He was on the point of admitting, to himself at least, that this spiteful act had been both cruel and ungrateful, but then he remembered the presence of Georges: 'Just as well for Georges to see what I'm really like, if he didn't know it already,' he thought. 'David Holm is not the man to give in that easily. He's tough and hard and enjoys upsetting sentimental fools.'

'I had not given much thought to the man's appearance until that moment,' the slum sister continued. 'But as he stood there tearing apart everything that Sister Edit had sewn with

54

many fine and godly thoughts, I studied him closely and saw that he was so tall and well-formed that it was impossible not to admire nature's handiwork. He carried himself easily, with a good, shapely head, and his face must once have been handsome. Now, however, it was blotched and swollen, its individual features blurred by decay and dissolution, so that there was no way of knowing what he had looked like originally.

'Although he did what he did, laughing loudly and wickedly as he did so, although his eyes flashed with an evil yellow gleam behind his red and swollen eyelids, I believe that Sister Edit only saw in him the splendour that was on the road to ruin. I saw how she drew back at first as if she had been struck, but then a clear light blazed in her eyes and she stepped towards him.

'The only words she spoke before he left were to ask him to come back to the refuge next New Year's Eve. He stood and looked at her, astonished and uncomprehending until she added: "You see, I prayed to Jesus last night. I prayed he would grant our first guest at the refuge a good New Year, and I want you to return so that I may see whether my prayer has been granted."

'When he understood what she meant, he responded with a loud oath. "Yes, I promise you," he said. "I'll come back and prove to you that He couldn't give a damn about you and your sentimental nonsense."'

Holm, thus reminded of a promise he had given and long forgotten, a promise which had nevertheless been fulfilled, felt for a moment as if he were a weak reed in the hand of a mightier power and wondered whether resistance was meaningless, but he stifled the thought: he would not submit, he would fight on until Doomsday if that was what it took.

The Salvationist soldier had become more and more agitated as Sister Maria spoke of this meeting on New Year's morning. Unable to stay quiet any longer, he leapt to his feet.

'You haven't mentioned the name of that down-and-out, Sister Maria, but I know it must have been David Holm.'

The slum sister nodded.

'My God, my God, Sister Maria!' he exclaimed, his hands held high. 'Why do you want me to bring him here? Has he become a better man since that morning? Has he? It's as if you want to bring him so that she will see that her prayers were in vain! Why do you want to cause her such distress?'

The slum sister looked at him, her impatience verging on anger.

'I haven't finished ...'

But the soldier interrupted her again.

'We must beware, Sister Maria, we must beware of falling into a desire for revenge. Sinful man that I am, I would like to bring David Holm here tonight so he could see her dying, and I would tell him that he is the one responsible for her leaving us. And I believe it is your intention to tell David Holm that Sister Edit caught the disease that is killing her while doing the work that he tore to shreds so ungratefully. You've said that Sister Edit has not enjoyed a single day of good health since last New Year's night. Those of us who have lived with Sister Edit and still have her before us must beware of allowing our hearts to grow hard.'

The slum sister bent forward over the table and spoke without raising her head, as if she were speaking to the figures on the tablecloth.

'Revenge,' she said. 'Is it revenge to make someone understand that he possessed something glorious and lost it? Is it revenge to put a rusty iron in the fire to make it clean and bright? Is that revenge?'

'That is what I thought, Sister Maria!' the soldier continued heatedly. 'You were hoping to convert David Holm by burdening his conscience with remorse. But have you considered that we may just be nurturing our own desire for vengeance? We are at risk of falling into that trap, Sister Maria. It is easy to stray from the path of righteousness.'

The pale slum sister looked at the soldier with eyes that shone with the light of self-denial. Her eyes carried the clear message: 'Tonight of all nights I am not seeking anything for myself.' Then, speaking with great emphasis, she said: 'There are many traps for us in a matter of this kind.'

The soldier's face flushed red as blood. He tried to answer but the words failed him. A moment later he flung himself down at the table and, overcome by pent-up sorrow, hid his face in his hands and began to weep.

The slum sister did not disturb him but her lips moved in prayer: 'O Lord God, Jesus Christ, bring us through the travails of this night! O Lord, in all my weakness and lack of understanding, grant me strength to help my friends!'

The bound and prostrate man had paid little attention to the accusation that he had infected Sister Edit, but the sight of the young soldier bursting into tears caused him to react violently. He had learnt something that affected him deeply and he did not bother to hide it from the driver: he was overjoyed that the woman the handsome young soldier loved had preferred him.

When the soldier's sobs grew less violent, the slum sister ceased praying and said gently: 'You're thinking of what I said a moment ago about Sister Edit and David Holm, aren't you, Gustavsson?'

With his head still buried in his arms, the soldier answered 'Yes', and his whole body trembled in pain.

'And it's causing you much suffering, I know,' she said. 'I know someone else who loved Sister Edit with their heart and soul. She noticed and said she could not understand it. She thought that if she were to care that much for someone, that someone would have to be better than her. And that's what you think, too, isn't it, Gustavsson? We may give our lives to the service of the wretched of the world, but we cannot give them our natural human love. When I tell you that Sister Edit's love is not like that, you will think that I am cheapening it, and you find that hurtful.'

The Salvationist did not move. He remained with his head on the table, but the invisible figure was trying to move closer, as if to hear better. Georges, however, told him to remain where he was.

'If you move, David, I shall have to punish you in a way you can't even dream of,' he said, and David Holm, who knew now that Georges would keep his word, remained motionless.

'Hallelujah!' the slum sister exclaimed, her face glowing with excitement. 'Hallelujah! What right do we have to judge her? You must have noticed, Gustavsson, that a heart that is filled with pride gives its love to the great and powerful of this world, but when a heart is filled with mercy and humility, who else can it give its warmest love to than to someone who has sunk to the depths of brutality, degradation and error?'

David Holm felt a stab of discomfort on hearing these words. 'You're in a strange mood tonight,' he thought. 'What do you care what these people say about you? Did you expect them to have any respect for you?'

The soldier raised his head from the table and looked hard and questioningly at the slum sister.

'It is not just that, Sister Maria.'

'I know, Gustavsson, I know what you mean. But bear in mind that when Sister Edit first met David Holm she did not know he was married. And, in any case,' she continued after a slight hesitation, 'I believe – and I cannot believe otherwise – that all of her love was aimed at converting him. If only she could have seen him step forward to the platform and confess that he was saved, she would have been happy.'

The Salvationist soldier grasped Sister Maria's hand and his eyes watched her lips as she spoke. On hearing these last words, he gave a deep sigh of relief and said: 'So it wasn't the sort of love that I thought!'

The slum sister raised her shoulders slightly and sighed at his obstinacy.

'Sister Edit has never confided anything to me about all this, so I may, of course, be mistaken.'

'Well, if you've never heard anything from Sister Edit's lips then, in my opinion, you are mistaken, Sister Maria,' the young man said very earnestly.

The ghost lying by the door thought the conversation was taking a gloomy turn.

'I'm not saying,' Sister Maria continued, 'that Sister Edit felt anything but compassion for David Holm the first time she saw him. And there was no reason for her to have loved him afterwards, either, since whenever she came across him, which was quite frequently for a time, he always defied her. Wives would come to us and complain that their husbands had been lured away from their jobs since Holm came to the town. And insolence, violence and vice all increased. Wherever we went among the poor, we heard the same story and we always seemed able to trace it back to David Holm. Being the woman she is, it was only natural for this to inspire Sister Edit to attempt to win him over for God. He was like a wild beast that she was fighting with all the weapons at her command, and the more he resisted her, the more fiercely she attacked, confident that she would be victorious in the end because she was the stronger of the two.'

'Hallelujah,' exclaimed the soldier, 'and so she was, Sister Maria, so she was. Do you remember how you and Sister Edit came into a drinking den one evening and went round handing out notices about your new slum refuge? Sister Edit saw a young man sitting there in Holm's company and the young man was listening and laughing as Holm made fun of the slum sisters. When she noticed that young man, Sister Edit's heart went out to him and she said a few words, telling him not to let himself be led into ruin. The young man did not answer her and he did not follow her immediately, but he could no longer bring himself to laugh, and although he stayed there in the same company and refilled his glass, he could no longer raise it to his lips. Holm and the others mocked him, saying that the slum sister had frightened him. But that is not what it was, Sister Maria, it was her compassion, the fact that she had felt she must warn him, that moved him and drove him to leave the others and follow her. You know that's true, Sister Maria, and you know who that young man was.'

'Amen, amen! Yes, I know who that man is and he has been the best of our friends ever since that day,' the slum sister said, inclining her head warmly to the soldier. 'I don't deny that Sister Edit occasionally got the better of Holm, but more often than not she failed. And she caught a chill that New Year's Night, with a cough that wouldn't go away – and still won't go away – however much she struggled. She has suffered the misery of sickness ever since and that, perhaps, is why she has been unable to fight the good fight with her old success.'

'Sister Maria,' the soldier said, 'there is nothing in what you have told me to suggest that Sister Edit is in love with Holm.'

'No, you are right. Nothing suggested it at the start. I'll tell you what convinced me that she is. We knew a poor seamstress who was struggling against tuberculosis, struggling above all not to spread the infection – she had a child she was trying to protect from the disease. She told us that one day she had been overcome by a fit of coughing in the street and a tramp had accosted her and criticised her fastidiousness. "I've got tuberculosis, too," he had said, "and the doctor has told me to be careful. But I'm not going to. I cough straight in people's faces because I hope they'll go down with it. Why should they be better off than us, that's what I'd like to know?"

'He had said no more than that but he frightened the seamstress so much that she felt ill all day. She described him as a tall man, who bore himself well in spite of being dressed in worthless rags. She had no clear memory of his face, but his eyes – two angry yellow slits between swollen eyelids – played on her mind for hours. What had really frightened her most, however, was that he spoke as he did, revealing such bitter hatred of his fellow-man, even though he did not appear to be drunk or completely derelict.

'It is no great surprise that Sister Edit immediately recognised David Holm from her description, but what amazed me was that she spoke up in his defence. She tried to convince the woman that he had found it amusing to scare her. "You must realise, don't you, that a man who looks that strong can hardly have tuberculosis," she said. "I think it was really nasty of him to want to frighten you, but he wouldn't go round infecting people on purpose if he really was ill. He is not such a monster as to do that."

'The rest of us disagreed. We thought he was as bad as he claimed to be, but she defended him more and more heatedly, almost becoming angry with us for believing the worst of him.'

For the second time the driver of the death cart showed that he was following everything going on around him. He bent down and looked into his companion's eyes. 'I think the slum sister is right, David. Someone who can refuse to believe all the evil in you must love you very much.'

The slum sister continued her account. 'Now it may be, Gustavsson, that all this meant nothing, and what I noticed a few days later perhaps meant even less. Sister Edit was walking home one evening, downcast and depressed by the setbacks afflicting those in her care, when David Holm appeared and began speaking to her. He just wanted to tell her, so he said, that she would be having a quieter and easier time of it since he was about to leave the town.

'I expected her to be pleased by this news, but from what she said to him in response I knew it made her unhappy. She told him directly that she would have preferred him to stay so that she could continue the struggle with him.

'He said he was sorry to hear that, but he had to go since he was about to travel round Sweden in search of someone he absolutely had to find. There would be no rest or peace for him until he found that person.

'And you know, Gustavsson, Sister Edit was so anxious to know who that person was that I was on the point of whispering to her that she should be careful not to waste herself on a man like that. Holm appeared not to notice, however, and simply answered that she would certainly hear about it if he found the person he was looking for. In which case he hoped she would be pleased that he no longer needed to roam round the country as a poor tramp.

'With that, he disappeared and he must have kept his word because we saw no more of him. I hoped that we'd never have anymore to do with him because he seemed to bring misfortune wherever he turned up. Then one day a woman arrived at the slum refuge, asking for Sister Edit and inquiring about David Holm. She said she was his wife and, unable to put up with his drinking and bad habits any longer, she had left him. She had gone secretly, taking their children with her, and moved to our town, which was so far away from their former home that it had never occurred to him to bother to look for her here. She had found work in a factory and was well enough paid to be able to support herself and the children. She was well-dressed and she inspired respect and confidence, having become a kind of supervisor of the young girls working in the factory. She had already earned enough to set up a comfortable home, properly fitted out and furnished. When she had still been living with Holm, however, there had never been enough money to feed her and the children and they had all gone hungry.

'But now she had heard that her husband had been seen in the town and that the slum sisters knew him. She had come to us to find out about him.

'If you'd been with us then, Gustavsson, and seen and heard Sister Edit, you'd have never forgotten it. When the woman told us who she was, the colour drained from Sister Edit's face and she looked as if she had suffered a mortal blow. She quickly pulled herself together and a light came into her eyes that can only be described as heavenly. It was as if she had overcome her own feelings and had no further desire for earthly things. She spoke to Holm's wife so tenderly that it moved her to tears. She did not reproach her, yet she caused her to repent of having deserted her husband. I think the woman began to see herself as guilty of great harshness and, what is more, Sister Edit seemed able to reawaken in her the old love she had felt for her husband when they were first married. She encouraged the woman to talk about how things had been in the early days of the marriage and she made her long for her husband. She certainly did not hide what he was like now, but she inspired in Holm's wife the same strong desire to reform him as she felt herself.'

During this speech the driver of the death cart once again bent down and looked at his prisoner, but this time he straightened up without saying anything. There was something so dark and dreadful about his former friend that he was unable to face it. He drew himself to his full height and pulled his cowl down over his eyes to avoid seeing him.

'Holm's wife must already have been feeling a germ of remorse for having abandoned her husband to his evil and wicked ways,' the slum sister continued. 'Talking to Sister Edit caused her remorse to grow, although on this first visit there was no suggestion that she should let her husband know where she was – that was decided during the long conversations they had later. I wouldn't like to say that Sister Edit convinced her to do so, or that she gave her any great hope, but I do know that she wanted her to take her husband back into her home. She believed it would be the salvation of him and she did nothing to dissuade her. I have to say that it was Sister Edit who made it happen, I have to say that she was the one who reunited the husband with the family he had the power to destroy. I have pondered on it a great deal and I do not believe she would have risked being responsible for all that unless she loved him.'

The slum sister spoke these words with great conviction, but the two men who had become so excited when she first spoke of the dying slum sister's love remained quiet. The Salvationist soldier sat motionless with his hands covering his eyes, and the face of the prostrate figure by the door had once again assumed the expression of bitter hatred it had revealed when he was first dragged into the room.

'None of us knew where David Holm had gone,' the slum sister continued her account. 'But Sister Edit spread the word among other tramps that we had information for him about his wife and children, and it wasn't long before he reappeared. Sister Edit arranged a meeting between him and his wife, having first found him a job as a building worker and seen to it that he was decently dressed. She didn't ask him to make any promises or to give any undertakings – she knew that people like him can't be bound with promises – she simply wanted to transplant into good soil the seed that had fallen among thorns. She was sure she would succeed.

'And who knows whether she might have been successful? But then our great misfortune struck and Sister Edit went down with inflammation of the lungs. When that was under control and we began to hope for a swift recovery, she went into decline and we had to send her to the sanatorium.

'I don't need to tell you, Gustavsson, how David Holm treated his wife – you know, and we all know. Sister Edit is the only one we have tried to keep in ignorance, because we want to spare her. We have been hoping she would die before she found out, but now I'm not so sure: I think she already knows.'

'How could she have found out?'

'The bonds that tie her to David Holm are so strong that I believe she could have become aware of it in ways beyond the ordinary human ways. It is because she knows that she has been asking all day to speak to him. She has brought endless misery to his wife and children and she has only a few hours left in which to put things right. And we are so useless that we cannot even help her by getting him to come here.'

'What good would it do, anyway?' the soldier asked stubbornly. 'She's too weak to talk to him.'

'I can talk to him in her name,' the slum sister said confidently. 'He would listen to the words said to him at her death-bed.'

'And what would you say to him, Sister Maria? Would you tell him that she loved him?'

The slum sister stood up and, with her hands together before her breast, turned her face towards Heaven and closed her eyes. She prayed.

'O Lord Our God, grant to us that David Holm comes here before Sister Edit dies! Almighty God, grant that he may see her love and that the fire of her love may melt his soul! Almighty God, was not that love given to her so that she may achieve victory over his heart? Almighty God, grant me the strength not to spare her but to have the courage to place his soul in the flame of her love! Almighty God, may he feel a gentle breeze pass through his soul like the breath of an angel's wings, like the red glow that kindles the dawn in the east and drives away the darkness of night! Almighty God, let him not believe that I seek vengeance on him! Almighty God, let him understand that Sister Edit has only loved the very essence of his soul, that which he himself has tried to smother and kill! Almighty God,

…'

The slum sister started and looked up. The Salvationist soldier was standing up and putting on his coat.

'I will go for him, Sister Maria,' he said, his voice thick with emotion. 'I will not return without him.'

But the prostrate figure by the door turned to the driver of the death cart and spoke: 'Georges, haven't we heard enough of this? When I arrived here, there was something in what they were talking about that touched me. If they had continued in that vein, I may have weakened. But you should have warned them – warned them not to talk about my wife.'

The driver did not answer him, instead he pointed quietly into the room. An old woman had entered through the door at the far end of the living room. With quiet steps she walked towards the two Salvationists and said in a voice that trembled with the import of what she had to say.

'She doesn't want to lie in there any longer. She wants to be moved out here. It will soon be over now.'

Thought
Similarities between Majores
in Gösta Berling and Slum Sister
— both strong women
— however — slum sister is a flawed
character — her weakness for David Holm
she persue his wife to get back to him
which results in her abuse

Sister Edit's
"point of view"

VI

The poor little slum sister lying on her death-bed felt herself becoming weaker with every moment that passed. No longer in any pain, she lay fighting death just as she had fought sleep during the many nights she had tended the sick.

'Oh, how sweet the temptation! But I must not succumb,' had been her thought then, and if sleep had overcome her for a few moments, she had quickly jumped up and returned to her duties.

Now, somewhere in a cool room where the air was pure and fresh and sweet for her sick lungs to breathe, she knew that a deep and broad bed was being prepared for her, a bed with pillows as soft and yielding as rising dough. She longed to sink into them and sleep away this endless weariness, but she knew that if she did she would sleep so deeply that she would never wake. So she fought the temptation to rest. Her time had not yet come.

There was a look of reproach in her eyes as she gazed out into the room. Her look was sterner than it had ever been.

Slum Sister "sense" Holm's presence

'How cruel you are not to help me with the one thing I desire,' she seemed to be complaining. 'Did I not do my utmost to serve you all when I was well, so why can't you take the trouble to summon the man I want to see now?'

She lay as she usually did with her eyes closed, waiting and listening so eagerly that not a sound or a movement in that little house escaped her. Suddenly she sensed that someone had come into the outer room and was waiting to be brought in to her. She opened her eyes and looked pleadingly at her mother.

'He's standing by the kitchen door. Can't you let him in, mother?'

Her mother got up, went to the door of the main room and opened it. She looked into the larger room and then came back, shaking her head.

'There is no one there, my child,' she said. 'Just Sister Maria and Gustavsson.'

The sick woman sighed and shut her eyes. Once again she sensed his presence just inside the door, waiting. If her clothes had been in their usual place on the chair at the foot of the bed, she would have tried to dress and go out to talk to him. But her clothes were not there and, in any case, she feared her mother would not have allowed her to get up.

She thought over and over how she could get to the other room. She was certain he was there and that her mother could not bring herself to let him in – after all, Mother must think that he looks dreadful and wouldn't want her talking to a man like that. Mother cannot see any point in her meeting him; Mother must think that since she is dying it makes no difference to her what happens to him now.

At last she came up with what seemed like a clever idea. 'I shall ask Mother to let me move into the large room and lie there,' she thought. 'I'll tell her I'm longing to see the room again. She can't have any objection to that.'

So she asked her mother, but she could not help wondering whether her mother had divined her reason for wanting to move.

'Aren't you comfortable where you are?' her mother asked. 'You've been quite happy in this room all the other days.'

Her mother just sat there and showed no sign of acceding to her request. The slum sister felt as if she was a child again, asking for something her mother did not approve of. And just like a small child she began to plead and nag in order to wear down her resistance.

'Mother, I really want to be in the big room. Gustavsson and Sister Maria can easily carry me through if you just call them. My bed won't have to stay there for long.'

'Once you are there, you will soon want to come back here,' her mother said, but she stood up and went to fetch the two Salvationists.

It was fortunate for the three of them – Gustavsson, Sister Maria and her mother – that she lay in the light wooden bed she had slept in as a child, and they had no difficulty in carrying her through. The moment she reached the doorway, she looked quickly towards the kitchen and was surprised not to see him. She had felt certain he would be there this time.

Bitterly disappointed, she closed her eyes again without looking round the three parts of the room, all of which held so many memories. And then, immediately, the sensation that someone was waiting over by the door returned to her. 'I can't possibly be mistaken,' she thought. 'There must be someone there, either him or someone else.'

She opened her eyes and scanned the room carefully. Straining hard, she sensed the presence of something over by the door. It was not as distinct as a shadow – more, she thought, like the shadow of a shadow.

Her mother bent down to her. 'Are you feeling better now that you are in here?' she asked.

Edit nodded and whispered that she was happy to be there. But she was not thinking of the room, she was watching the door the whole time. 'What is over there? What is it?' she wondered. Finding out what it was meant more than life itself.

Sister Maria moved and blocked her view of the door. Summoning all of her strength, Edit managed to make her move away. They had placed her bed in the part of the room furnished as the parlour. It was farthest from the door and after she had lain there for a while, she whispered to her mother: 'Now I've seen what the parlour looks like, I'd like to move to the dining room.'

She saw the worried look her mother exchanged with the other two and she saw them shake their heads. She interpreted it as meaning that they were worried about moving her closer to the shadowy presence by the door. Little by little, she had begun to suspect who it was and she was not afraid, she just wanted to be closer to him.

She gave her mother and her friends a pleading look and they moved her without any further objections.

The part of the room that served as a dining room was much closer to the door and now she could discern a dark form standing there with some kind of implement in his hands. That could not be him, but it was vital that she met whoever it was.

She had to get closer. With a great effort, she forced an apologetic smile and made a sign that she would like to be moved to the kitchen. She could see that her mother was so upset by all this that she had begun to weep. The thought crossed her mind that her mother was remembering how she used to sit on the floor in front of the stove, her face glowing in the firelight as she chatted about everything that had happened in school while her mother prepared their supper. She realised that her mother was seeing her in all of her ordinary old places and was beginning to be overwhelmed by a sense of impending emptiness. But she must not think of her mother now, must not think of anything but the task she needed to accomplish in the short time she had left.

Once they had moved her to the kitchen end of the room, she could at last pick out the vague shape by the door. She could see a figure in a black cloak with a hood pulled forward over his face and with a long scythe in his hand, and she could no longer be in any doubt as to who it was.

'That is Death,' she thought, feeling no fear other than that he had come to fetch her too soon.

As the sick woman's bed was gradually moved closer, the bound and prostrate figure on the floor curled up and tried to make himself smaller to avoid being seen. He noticed how she kept looking towards the door as if she could see something there. He did not want her to catch sight of him – the humiliation would be too much to bear. But her eyes did not meet his, they were focused on someone else, and he realised that if she was aware of a presence, it was not him, but Georges.

Once she had been moved close to the door, Holm noticed that she was making a small sign with her head, calling Georges

69

to come to her bedside. Georges drew his cloak tighter round him as though he were cold and approached her. She looked up at him with a little smile.

'You can see that I'm not afraid of you,' she whispered almost inaudibly. 'I will willingly answer your call. But I must ask you to grant me one more day to allow me to accomplish the great task for which God sent me into this world.'

While she was talking to Georges, Holm raised his head to look at her. He saw that the holy sublimity of her spirit had endowed her with a beauty she had not possessed before; there was something proud and lofty and unattainable about her, but so irresistible that he found it impossible to take his eyes from her.

'Can you hear me?' she asked Georges. 'Bend a little closer. I must speak to you without the others hearing what I say.'

Georges bent forward so that his cowl was almost touching her face.

'Speak as quietly as you like,' he said. 'I shall still hear you.'

She then began to speak in a whisper so weak that none of the three people around her bed were aware that she was talking. Only the driver and his ghostly companion could hear her.

'I don't know if you understand how much is at stake for me,' she said to Georges, 'but I must be given until tomorrow. There is someone I must meet so that I can bring him to the paths of righteousness. You cannot know how badly I have acted, how self-willed and reckless I have been. How can I stand before God, I, who am the cause of such dreadful misfortune?'

Her eyes grew wide with fear and she struggled for breath, but then continued without waiting for an answer.

'I must tell you that the man I want to meet is the man I love. You understand me, don't you? The man I love.'

'But Sister Edit,' the driver answered, 'that man ...'

She did not want to hear his answer before she had been allowed to tell him everything that might move him.

'You understand that I am in dire need when I tell you this. It is not easy for me to confess to loving that man. I have been filled with shame at my wickedness in loving someone who is bound to another. I have struggled and fought to resist. I, who should be a beacon and example to the wretched, feel that I have become worse than the worst of them.'

Georges said nothing, but he gently stroked her brow to calm her before letting her continue.

'But the worst humiliation is not that I love a married man. The real degradation lies in me loving a man who is wicked and evil. I don't know why I came to throw myself away on a worthless wretch. I have hoped and believed I would find some goodness in him but I have always been deceived. How wicked I must be for my heart to go so far astray. Can't you see that it is impossible for me to leave this world without being given the chance to make one more attempt, without seeing him change into a better man?' -

'You have already made many attempts, haven't you?' Georges said in a doubtful tone.

She closed her eyes and thought things over, but then she looked up, her face shining with renewed confidence.

'You think I am asking this for my own sake and, like everyone else, you believe that what happens to him can make no difference to me as I am about to be taken from all earthly concerns. Please let me tell you about something that happened today – this very day – and you will understand that the reason I need more time is so that I can help others.'

She closed her eyes and continued speaking without opening them again.

'It was this morning. I don't understand how, but somehow I found myself out and about with a basket of food to feed the poor. Suddenly I was standing in a yard where, as far as I know, I had never been before. There were tall houses all round me and they looked respectable and well-cared for, as if the people living there were quite well-off. I had no idea what I was supposed to be doing in this place, but then I noticed an outbuilding against the wall of one of the houses – it looked as though it had been built as a hen-house. Someone had tried to turn it into a home: planks and cardboard had been nailed on

Attonement – she (Sister Edit) wants to attone for her sins? (David Holm's wife)

here and there, there were two or three crooked windows, and a couple of metal chimney pipes had been fixed on the roof.

'A thin column of smoke was rising from one of the chimneys, and when I realised someone was living there, I said to myself that this must be where I was to go.

'I went up some wooden steps – they were as steep as a ladder and I had the feeling I was climbing up to some kind of bird's nest – and put my hand on the latch. It was unlocked and, hearing voices inside, I walked in without knocking.

'No one turned round to look at me when I entered and I drew back into a corner by the door to wait until I was needed. For I knew with absolute certainty that I had come there for some vital purpose.

'Meanwhile, I stood there with the feeling of being in an outhouse rather than in a room where people lived. There was hardly any furniture, not even a bed, just a couple of ragged mattresses thrown in one corner to serve as beds. No chairs – at any rate, no chairs that even a rag and bone merchant would bother with – and only a rough unpainted table.

'All at once it came to me where I was. The woman standing there was David Holm's wife, and his family had obviously moved while I was in the sanatorium. But why were they living in such poverty and discomfort? Where was their furniture? Where was the beautiful bureau, and the sewing machine and …?

'I stopped counting. There was no point in counting the things that were missing, since nothing was left.

'She looked utterly despairing, I thought. And so poorly dressed. Not at all like the woman she had been last spring. I wanted to rush up to her and ask, but I held back because there were two unfamiliar women in the room and the three of them were involved in conversation.

'All three were talking earnestly and I soon understood what the issue was. Their father had tuberculosis and the intention was to remove the poor woman's children to a children's home to avoid the danger of infection.

'I could scarcely believe what I was hearing. David Holm

can't have tuberculosis, I thought. I had heard it rumoured before but could not bring myself to believe it.

'I was puzzled, too, by the fact that they were only talking about two children. I seemed to remember that there were three. It was not long before I learnt why. One of the good women noticed that the mother was crying and said some kind words about the children being as well cared for as they would be at home.

'"Pay no attention to my tears, doctor," I heard Holm's wife say. "I would weep even more if I couldn't send the children away. My youngest is already in hospital and when I saw his suffering I said I would be more than thankful to get the other two out of the house."

'On hearing this, my heart filled with anxiety. What had David Holm done to his wife, his children and his home? Or, to be more precise, what had I done to them? After all, I was the one who had brought them back together.

'Standing there in the corner, I began to sob. I couldn't understand why they had not noticed me, but none of them seemed aware of my presence.

'I saw Holm's wife go to the door. "I'm just going down to the street to call the children," she said. "They're not far away."

'She walked past me, so close that her poor, patched dress brushed against my hand. I fell to my knees with tears in my eyes, pressed the cloth to my lips and kissed it. There was nothing I could say – the wrong I had done this woman was too great for words. I was surprised that she did not seem to see me, but I could certainly understand why she would not want to speak to me after I had brought such misfortune to her home.

'The poor woman did not leave the room, however, since one of the women said there was another matter to be dealt with before fetching the children. She took a document from her handbag and read it out. It was the official form giving her custody of the children for as long as their home was infected with tuberculosis. Both father and mother had to sign.

'There was a door at the other end of the room. It opened

and David Holm entered. I couldn't help thinking that he must have been listening behind the door and waiting for the right moment to make his entrance.

'He was wearing the same filthy old clothes and there was a malevolent look in his eyes. There is no denying the fact that he looked round with obvious satisfaction, as if he was pleased to see all this misery.

'He began saying how much he loved his children and how hard it would be to lose the other two when one child was already in hospital. The two women hardly bothered to listen to him. They merely pointed out that he was much more likely to lose his children unless he was prepared to send them away.

'While they were telling him this I looked from him to his wife, who had retreated against the wall and was looking at him, I thought, as someone who has been whipped and racked might look at her torturer. I began to realise that my actions had been even more unjust than I had thought. It seemed to me that David Holm nursed some kind of secret hatred of this woman – that his desire to be reunited with her had arisen not from his longing for a home but so that he could continue tormenting her.

'I listened to him standing there regaling the two well-off women with protestations of fatherly love. They answered that the surest proof of that love would be to follow the doctor's advice and avoid spreading his infection around. In which case they would be quite happy to see the children remain at home.

'Neither of the women had any idea what he had in mind. I was the first to recognise it. "He intends to hang on to the children," I thought. "He doesn't care if they catch the disease."

'But his wife quickly saw the same thing and uttered a violent scream: "He's a murderer! He doesn't want me to send them away, he wants to keep them here to infect them so that they die too! He thinks he can take revenge on me by killing them!"

'Holm shrugged his shoulders and turned his back on her. "She is right, I don't want to sign that paper," he said to the two women. And he stood there, calmly assuring them that he could not live without his children.

'I listened in a state of indescribable anguish. None of them could have been suffering as I was suffering since none of them loved the man who was committing this crime. I stood there praying they would find the right words to soften his heart. I felt like rushing forward, but, in some strange way, I was held fast in the corner. "There is no point in arguing with him," I thought. "The only way with a man like that is to frighten him." None of the three women said a word about the Almighty. None of them threatened him with the wrath of a righteous God. I felt I was holding God's avenging thunderbolt in my hand but was powerless to hurl it.

'The room fell silent. The two ladies rose and prepared to leave. They had achieved nothing. Nor had Holm's wife. She had given up the struggle and collapsed in despair. Once again I made a superhuman effort to move and to speak. The words were burning on my tongue. "Oh, you hypocrite!" I wanted to say. "Do you think I can't see what you really intend? I, who am dying, summon you to meet me before God's judgment seat. Before God, the Supreme Judge, I shall accuse you of wanting to murder your children. I shall bear witness against you."

'But as I stepped forward to say these words, I found that I was no longer in David Holm's room, I was here at home, lying powerless in my bed. Ever since then I have called and called, but could not get him to come to me.'

The little slum sister had been lying with her eyes closed as she whispered this story to Georges. Now her eyes opened wide and a look of fearful anguish came to her face. 'You cannot let me die without speaking to him,' she pleaded. 'Think of his children. Think of his wife.'

The figure on the floor marvelled at Georges. He could have calmed her with a few words, he could have told her that David Holm was now no more and no longer capable of harming his wife and children, but he withheld the news and went on instead to add to her suffering.

'What power could you hope for over David Holm?' he said. 'He is not a man whose heart can be moved. What you saw today was nothing but the vengeance his heart has rejoiced in planning for many a long year.'

'Oh, don't say that, don't say that!' Sister Edit exclaimed.

'I know him better than you know him,' the driver said. 'And I shall tell you what made David Holm into the man he is.'

'I should like you to tell me,' she said. 'It would be so good to understand him.'

'Then you must come with me to another town, where we will stand outside a prison cell. It is evening and a man who has been in for a week or two for drunkenness has just been released. There is no one waiting for him at the prison gate, although he stops and looks around in the hope of someone coming. He has been hoping so much that someone will be there.

'The man coming out of prison is in great distress. While he was inside, his younger brother committed a serious crime – he killed a man in a drunken rage and is now in prison himself. The older brother knew nothing of this until the prison chaplain took him to the killer's cell, where he saw his younger brother still in handcuffs after violently resisting arrest. "Can you see who that is?" the chaplain asked. The man was profoundly affected by the sight of the brother, of whom he had always been so fond. "He will be the one to stay in prison for many years," the chaplain said. "But all of us here think that you, David Holm, should be serving his sentence for him, since you – you alone – are the one who tempted him and led him astray until he became such a drunkard that he had no idea what he was doing."

'It is all Holm can do to remain calm until he is back in his own cell, when he begins to weep as he has not wept since he was a child. And he promises himself that he will change and turn away from his wicked past. He had never before imagined how it would feel to bring such misery to someone he loved. Then his thoughts turn from his brother to his wife and children; he sees that they, too, have suffered greatly and he promises himself that they will never again have cause to complain. Thus, as he leaves prison in the evening light, he is longing for his wife to be there so that he can tell her that he will be a different man.

'But she is not there to meet him at the prison gates, nor does he meet her along the road. When he arrives at their home and knocks on the door, she does not open the door to him as she usually does when he has been absent for a long time. The truth of the situation begins to dawn on him, but he refuses to believe it. This cannot be happening now, not when he has resolved to change and become a different man.

'His wife usually leaves the key hidden under the doormat when she goes out. He bends down and finds it in its customary place. He opens the door, looks in and wonders whether he has come to the wrong place since the room is empty. Most of the furniture remains, but there is no sign of a living soul. Nor is there wood for the fire, food in the cupboard or curtains at the windows. The room is bleak and comfortless and has not been lived in for several days.

'He goes to the neighbours and asks whether his wife has fallen ill while he was away. He tries to persuade himself that she has been taken to hospital. "No, there was nothing the matter with her when she left," they answer. "Where did she go?" No one knows.

'Their answers revealed a mixture of nosiness and malicious glee and he realised that there could only be one explanation. His wife had taken her chance to leave him while he was in prison. She had taken the children and anything else she needed, leaving him to come home to this unexpected emptiness. And he had been thinking he would come to her and bring her great joy. He had even been rehearsing what he would say to her, how he would beg her forgiveness. He had a friend, a man who had once belonged to a better class of society but who was now utterly dissolute; henceforth he intended to avoid the company of this man, whose appeal lay not only in his wickedness but also in his culture and knowledge. He had been intending to go to his old employer the next day and ask for his job back. He would have worked like a slave for his wife and children, toiled so that they could wear decent clothes and never endure another day's worry. But while he had been thinking all this, she had deserted him.

'His blood ran hot and cold and he shuddered at her heartlessness. He could have understood her leaving him if she had done so openly and honestly. In that case, he would have had no right to be angry since he had given her a hard life. But to have crept away, leaving him to return to an empty home with no word of warning, that was heartless. He could never forgive her for that.

'She had put him to shame in front of everyone. She had made him the laughing stock of the neighbourhood, and he swore to himself that he would put a stop to their laughter. He would find his wife and he would make her unhappy – as unhappy as he was, and even more so. He would teach her what it felt like to have the very core of your heart turned to ice, as she had done to him. The only thing that comforted him was the thought of how he would punish her when he found her.

'He spent three years hunting for her, all the time nourishing his hatred by dwelling on what she had done to him until it seemed a crime of unimaginable proportion. All alone he tramped the lonely roads, and all the while his hatred and lust for revenge grew stronger. And during his long search, he had ample time to plan how he would torment her if they should ever be reunited.'

The little slum sister had remained silent throughout this account though her face showed she was following every word attentively. Now, however, with an anxious voice, she interrupted the dark figure.

'Oh no, don't tell me any more! It's too horrible. How can I ever answer for what I've done? Oh, if only I hadn't brought them back together! Had I not done so, his sins would never have grown so great.'

'I shall say no more, then,' the driver replied. 'I just want you to recognise that it would serve no purpose to ask for more time.'

'Oh, but I need it!' she exclaimed anxiously. 'I cannot die yet, I cannot! Give me just a few moments. You know I love him, and

I have never loved him as much as I do today.'

The ghostly presence by the door gave a start. Throughout the whole of the conversation between Sister Edit and the driver, he had been watching her. He had hungrily taken in every word she said, every expression that crossed her face, so that he might remember them forever. Everything she had said, even the harshest things, had sounded sweet to his ears, and all her anxiety and compassion when Georges told her his story was balm to his wounds. As yet he could hardly put his feelings for her into words, but he knew that he could bear any burden she laid upon him. He saw that her love for him – for a man who had been as he had been, for a man who had brought death to her – was wondrous in its sublimity. Each time she said she loved him, his soul rejoiced in ecstasy. He attempted to attract Georges' attention, but the driver was not looking at him. He tried to rise, but fell back in unspeakable pain.

He saw how Sister Edit was tossing and turning anxiously and restlessly in her bed as she reached out to Georges, her hands clenched imploringly in prayer. But the driver's face remained stern and implacable.

'I would give you time if time were of any help,' he said to her. 'But I know you have no power over that man.' And the driver bent forward to utter the words that would release her soul from its earthly clay.

At that moment a dark figure struggled across the floor towards the dying woman. With agonising effort, enduring pain beyond anything he had ever imagined, Holm had torn himself free from his bonds to draw near her. Although certain now that he was condemned to suffer this agony for all eternity, he could no longer bear the knowledge that he was present in the room where Sister Edit was waiting in vain for him to come. He crawled to the other side of the bed, hidden from Georges' hostile eyes, until he was close enough to take Sister Edit by the hand.

Though it was impossible for him to press her hand, she was aware of his presence and, with a quick movement, turned towards him. She saw David Holm kneeling at her side with his face pressed to the floor, not daring to look up at her. Only the hand that touched hers told her of his love, his gratitude, and the gentle melting of his heart.

A glow of ineffable bliss suffused the dying woman's face. She looked up at her mother and at her two friends, to whom she had been too preoccupied until now to bid farewell, and she wanted them to partake in the miracle that had happened to her. She pointed down for them to witness David Holm lying at her feet and to share her eternal joy in his contrition and remorse. But the cloaked figure of Georges stepped forward and said:

'Thou captive, thou dearly beloved, depart from thy cell.'

Sister Edit lay back on her pillows and her life left her with a sigh.

At that same moment David Holm was snatched away. His legs remained free, but he felt the invisible bonds tightening again round his arms. In an angry whisper Georges let him know that their old friendship was the only thing that had prevented him being punished with eternal suffering.

'Come with me now!' Georges continued. 'You and I have no business here. Those who are to welcome her have arrived.'

He dragged David Holm violently out of the room. Holm thought he saw the room filling with bright figures, and they were present on the steps, too, and out in the street. But he was dragged away at such a giddying speed that he could perceive nothing clearly.

VII

David Holm was lying in the death cart, where he had been thrown, angry not only with the world around him, but also with himself. What kind of madness had come over him? What had led him to fall at Sister Edit's feet like a remorseful and penitent sinner? Georges must be laughing at him. A real man should stand by his actions – after all, he knows why he committed them. He was not the man to throw everything overboard just because a slip of a girl said she was in love with him. What on earth had taken hold of him? Was it love? But he was dead. And she was dead. What kind of love could that be?

The lame horse was moving again, plodding along one of the roads that led out of town. The houses were becoming fewer and the street lamps farther apart. They were in sight of the town boundary, after which there were no more lights.

As they approached the last lamp-post, Holm was engulfed by a sudden feeling of grief, an inexplicable sense of distress at leaving the town. He felt he was being taken away from something he should never leave.

As this came over him, he heard the sound of voices. He raised his head to hear them over the dreadful screeching and rattling of the cart. Georges was talking to someone, someone who seemed to be in the cart with them, another passenger, whose presence he had been unaware of.

'I can go with you no farther,' a gentle voice was saying, so muffled by sorrow and suffering that it was scarcely audible. 'I had so much to say to him, but he is so full of anger and evil that I can't make him see me or hear me. You must carry my words to him and tell him that I came to meet him, but that I am now being taken away and will not be permitted to reveal myself again in my present form.'

'And if he reforms and shows remorse?' Georges said.

'You said yourself that he is beyond reform,' the voice said, trembling with sorrow. 'You must tell him that I believed that we belonged together for eternity, but from this moment on he will never see me again.'

'And if he atones for his evil deeds?' Georges said.

'You must tell him that I can accompany him no further than this,' the voice said mournfully. 'Tell him that I said farewell.'

'And if he changes utterly, if he becomes a different man?'

'You may tell him that I shall always love him,' the voice said with even more sadness than before. 'That is the only hope I have to offer him.'

David Holm had risen to his knees on the bottom of the cart. When he heard these words, he struggled with all his might and rose to his full height. He reached out to grasp at something, but it fluttered away from his bound and fumbling hands. He could not make out what it was, but it left an impression of something bright and shimmering, of beauty that surpassed all imagination.

He wanted to tear himself free and hurry after it, but he was hindered by something that tied him more firmly than fetters. Once again, as at the bedside, he was overwhelmed by love, that spiritual love, of which human love is at best a poor imitation. The warmth of love was beginning to glow within him, burning slowly and hardly perceptibly at first, like wood catching in a newly kindled fire, the transient flame hinting at the blaze to come. A flame now flickered in David Holm, not yet burning brightly, but shedding light enough for him to see the one he loved in such glory that he sank down helpless, overcome by the knowledge that he could not and dared not draw near her.

VIII

The driver drove onwards through the darkness. On both sides of the narrow road the trees of the forest stood so tall and dense that the sky was invisible. In the forlorn monotony of this place, the horse seemed to be moving more slowly and the screech of the wheels became more piercing, and all the while the mind's inquisition of the soul grew sterner. Then Georges pulled on the reins, the screech of the wheels ceased and he cried in a ringing voice:

'What is all the torment I am suffering, what is all the torment that awaits me, compared to the fact that I no longer live in uncertainty about the one thing that matters to me? I thank Thee, O God, that I have come from the darkness of earthly life. In all my misery I praise and glorify Thee because I know that Thou hast given me the gift of eternal life.'

The journey continued, accompanied by the jolts and screeches of the cart, but the driver's words lingered in Holm's ears. For the first time he felt compassion for his old friend. 'He is a brave man,' he thought. 'He does not complain even though there is no hope of him escaping his duties.'

*

It was a long journey they undertook, a journey that seemed without end.

They had been on the road for what Holm reckoned to be a full day and a night when they came to a wide plain, where the sky above was no longer overcast and a gleaming half-moon shone between Orion's Belt and the Seven Sisters.

83

Slowly, oh so slowly, the lame horse plodded across the plain and when, at last, they had crossed it, Holm peered up at the moon to see how far they had travelled. To his amazement he discovered that they had made no progress at all.

They drove on and at long intervals he glanced up at the sky, only to see that the moon remained motionless in its place between Orion's Belt and the Seven Sisters. He realised then that although he felt they had been travelling a day and a night, night had not turned to day and day had not turned to evening: the same night reigned the whole time. For what seemed like hours, they journeyed onward, but the hands on the great timepiece of the firmament remained motionless.

Had Holm not recalled Georges' words that time stretched and extended to enable the driver to come to all the places he needed to reach, he would have been tempted to believe that the earth had faltered in its orbit. He trembled at the thought that what, for him, had now become long days and nights were no more than a few short minutes by mankind's reckoning. He remembered how as a child he had been told of a man who had visited the afterlife and on his return the man had said that a century in God's heaven passed as quickly as one day on earth. So, for the driver of the death cart perhaps, one day was like a hundred years on earth.

Once again Holm felt a stirring of compassion for Georges. 'It's little wonder he is longing to be released,' he thought. 'It's been a long year for him.'

*

They were driving up a long hill when a woman, moving even more slowly than they were, came into view. They soon caught up with her.

She was an old woman, frail and bent, who was struggling along with the help of a stout stick. In spite of her frailty, she was carrying a bundle so heavy that it pulled her over to one side. It was clear that the old woman was able to see the death cart since she moved over to the side of the road and stood on the verge when it drew level with her. Then she increased her pace a little in order to walk alongside it, all the while studying it carefully to see what kind of carriage it was.

In the bright moonlight she soon realised that the horse was an ancient, one-eyed nag, that the harness consisted of withies and pieces of string knotted together, that the carriage was a cart so worn-out that both its wheels seemed likely to fall off at any moment.

'I can't understand why anyone would choose to travel round in a thing like that behind a horse that is on its last legs,' she muttered to herself without any thought that the travellers might be able to hear her. 'I was going to ask for a lift, but the horse has got enough to do as it is and the cart looks as if it would collapse if I climbed aboard.'

No sooner were the words out of her mouth than Georges leaned forward and began to sing the praises of his conveyance.

'This horse and cart are not as bad as you think. I have driven them across stormy seas where the waves were as tall as houses and great ships were sent to the bottom, and yet I did not capsize.'

The old woman was rather taken aback by this, but assuming she was just dealing with a droll sort of driver, she was quick to respond: 'I imagine you would be better off on a stormy sea, given the trouble you seem to be having making any progress on land.'

'I have driven down mine-shafts into the bowels of the earth and my horse has not stumbled – and I have driven through the furnace heat of burning cities with fire on every side. The world has not seen the fireman who would risk going as far into fire and smoke as this beast will go.'

'You think you can make a fool of an old woman, don't you, driver?' the woman said.

'I have sometimes had tasks that took me among high and trackless mountains,' the driver continued, 'and this horse has climbed precipices and traversed dangerous abysses. The cart has never let me down, even when the ground has been little more than a boulder-field. We have crossed swamps where there was no tussock firm enough to bear the weight of a child. Snowdrifts deep enough to bury a man upright have failed to stop us. I have no reason to complain about my horse and cart.'

'Well, if what you say is true, I'm not surprised you are satisfied,' the old woman said. 'You must be an important fellow to have such a grand carriage.'

'I am the mighty one who has power over the children of men,' the driver answered in a voice that was both sonorous and earnest. 'I command them all, whether they dwell in grand halls or miserable hovels. I bring freedom to slaves and I drag kings from their thrones. There is no fortress so mighty that I cannot scale its walls; there is no knowledge so profound that it can arrest my progress. I strike the confident even while they bask in their good fortune and I bestow riches on the downtrodden who are tormented by their poverty.'

'Just as I thought,' the old woman said with a laugh, 'I'm obviously lucky to have met an important man like you. Now, since you are so mighty and have such a splendid carriage, perhaps you would let me ride with you for a while? I set off to visit one of my daughters on New Year's Eve, but I got lost and I think I'll be tramping the roads all night unless you help me.'

'You must not ask that of me,' the driver said. 'Better to be tramping the road all night than riding on my cart.'

'I daresay you're right,' the old woman answered. 'Your horse looks as if it would drop if it had to carry me, too. But you could at least help me by letting me put my bundle up on the cart.'

Without waiting for permission, she quickly lifted up her bundle and put it on the cart but, just as if she had placed it on a billowing cloud of smoke or on a moving wall of mist, it fell straight to the ground.

At that moment she must have lost her ability to see the cart, for she remained standing bewildered and trembling in the middle of the road, and she made no further effort to talk to the driver.

This conversation once more stirred Holm's compassion for Georges. 'He has certainly had much to endure,' he thought. 'Little wonder he has changed.'

IX

The driver had brought David Holm into a room with tall, barred windows and bright but bare walls, devoid of any kind of decoration. Along one of the walls stood a row of beds, only one of which was occupied. A faint smell of medication met them when they entered. A warder was sitting by the bed and Holm realised that he was in a prison hospital.

By the light of a small electric lamp on the ceiling Holm could see that the bed was occupied by a sick young man with a handsome but emaciated face. As soon as he caught sight of the prisoner, Holm's earlier fury returned and he forgot any sympathy he had felt for Georges.

'What's he doing here?' he shouted, on the point of attacking Georges. 'If you do anything to him,' he said, pointing to the man in the bed, 'we will be enemies forever! Understand?'

The driver turned to him with compassion rather than sternness: 'I know now who the man in the bed is, David. I didn't know when we came in.'

'It's all the same to me whether you knew it or not, as long as you understand …'

He stopped abruptly. Georges had done no more than make a commanding gesture with his hand and, filled with sudden, irresistible fear, Holm fell silent.

'For you and for me,' the driver said, 'there is no choice but to submit and obey. It is not for you to desire or demand – only to wait quietly for understanding to come.'

Georges drew his cowl down over his face as a sign that he wished neither to hear nor to say any more, and in the silence that followed, Holm heard the sick prisoner speak to the warder.

'Do you think I will pull through?' he asked in a weak voice, but with no sign of despondency or sadness.

'Heavens above, of course you will,' the officer said kindly if a little uncertainly. 'You just need to buck up a bit and shake off this fever.'

'You know, don't you, that it wasn't the fever I was thinking of,' the sick man said. 'I was wondering whether you think I'll ever get my life back. It won't be easy after doing time for manslaughter.'

'You have got somewhere to go, Holm, so things will work out. At least you've always said you have a place where you'll be welcome.'

The man in the bed gave a radiant smile.

'How did the doctor think I was doing tonight?'

'Nothing to worry about, nothing at all. The doctor always says that once he gets you outside these walls, he'll soon have you up and about.'

The prisoner breathed in deeply, sucking the air between his teeth.

'Yes, outside these walls,' he whispered.

'I'm only repeating what the doctor always says,' the prison officer continued. 'But don't take him literally and disappear as you did last autumn. That just means a longer sentence, do you understand?'

'You don't need to worry about that. I've learnt my lesson and the only thing I think about now is getting my sentence over with. Then it will be time to start a new life.'

'You're right there, Holm, it will be a new life,' the warder said, and there was something solemn in the tone of his voice.

During this conversation David Holm was in greater pain than the sick man.

'They have let him catch the disease in prison,' he muttered, rocking backwards and forwards in his anguish. 'Now he's finished, and he was so fine-looking, so happy, so strong!'

'Officer …' the sick man began, but then, noticing the warder make a small gesture of impatience, quickly asked: 'Is it against regulations for me to talk so much?'

'No, you may talk as much as you like tonight, Holm.'

'Tonight? Is that because it's New Year's Night?' the prisoner asked thoughtfully.

'Yes, because a good New Year is beginning for you,' the officer answered.

'The warder fellow knows he is going to die tonight,' the prisoner's brother thought, stricken by his powerlessness to intervene. 'That's why he is being so kind to him.'

The prisoner returned to the question he had been meaning to ask: 'You must have noticed a change in me since I went on the run? I've kept out of trouble ever since, haven't I?'

'You've been like a lamb ever since you came back in. I've had no reason to complain. But as I said before – don't do it again!'

The sick man gave a smile and asked: 'Have you ever wondered why I changed, or did you think it was just because my illness has got worse since then?'

'Well, I suppose we assumed something of the sort.'

'But that's not the reason at all,' the prisoner said. 'It's something quite different. I haven't dared talk about it before, but tonight I'd like to tell you.'

'I really am afraid that you are talking too much, Holm,' the warder said. But when he saw the disappointed look on the sick man's face, he said gently: 'It's not that I'm getting tired of you talking, I'm just thinking of what's best for you.'

'Didn't you all think it was strange that I returned to prison of my own accord? None of you had any idea where I was, but I went to the police station and turned myself in of my own free will. Have you wondered why I did such an unlikely thing?'

'We thought you had probably been having such a rough time that you thought it best to give yourself up.'

'It's true that I had a hard time the first few days. But I was out for a good three weeks. Did you all think I was living wild in the forest all that time – in the middle of winter, too?'

'We had no reason to believe anything else, since that's what you told us.'

The prisoner looked as if he was enjoying himself.

'You have to fool the authorities sometimes to make sure that the people who helped you don't get into trouble. You wouldn't want that on your conscience, would you? Anyone brave enough to take in a man on the run and look after him deserves to be protected as much as you can. You wouldn't disagree with that, would you?'

'Now you are asking me things I couldn't possibly answer,' the warder said with the same patient tolerance he had shown all along.

The young prisoner heaved a deep sigh of longing: 'If I can only hold out until I get out of here again. There are some people living right on the edge of the forest ...'

He broke off and lay fighting for breath. The warder watched him anxiously, then he reached for the bottle of medicine. Seeing it was empty, he rose to his feet.

'I'll have to go and fetch some more of this,' he said and left the room.

The driver immediately took his place at the bedside, having first pushed his hood back and placed his scythe where the sick man could not see it.

David Holm burst into tears like a weeping child when he saw the dread figure of Georges so close to his brother, but his brother showed no sign of disquiet. Suffering as he was from a high fever, he thought that the prison warder had returned to his seat at the bedside.

'It was just a tiny cottage,' he said, panting with effort at every word.

'Don't tire yourself talking,' the driver said. 'The authorities already know everything that is in your thoughts, although we've been pretending not to.'

The sick man's eyes opened wide in astonishment.

'You're looking at me in bewilderment, young man,' the driver said, 'so I'll tell you. Did you think that we didn't know all about an escaped prisoner creeping up to a little cottage – the one at the end of the row in a long village – when he thought no one was at home. He had been lying in the edge of the trees waiting for the woman of the house to go out, because he assumed that her husband would be at work and he'd seen no sign of any children. When the woman went out with a milk-can on her arm, the fugitive watched carefully where she put the key and then he slipped into the cottage.'

'But how can you know that?' the sick man said, so surprised that he tried to sit up in bed.

'Just lie still, Holm,' the driver said in a kindly voice, 'and don't be concerned about your friends. Prison warders are human beings, too, you know. Let me tell you what I know. When that fugitive crept into the cottage, he got a fright, because it wasn't as empty as he had thought. A sick child was lying there watching him from a big bed over by the far wall. Very quietly, he walked over to the child, who quickly closed his eyes and played dead.

'"Why are you in bed in the middle of the day?" the fugitive asked. "Are you ill?" The child did not move. "You don't need to be afraid of me," the man said. "Just tell me where I can get some food and I'll be on my way as soon as possible."

'When the child still lay motionless and refused to answer, the intruder pulled a straw out of the mattress and tickled the boy's nose, which made him sneeze. That made the man laugh and the child, after at first staring at him in amazement, also began to laugh. "I thought I'd pretend to be dead," the boy said. "I could see that – but what was it supposed to achieve?" "Don't you know that if you meet a bear in the forest you should throw yourself to the ground and pretend to be dead? When the bear goes off to dig a pit to put you in, you can escape."

'The intruder blushed. "So you thought I was going to dig a pit to put you in, did you?" he said. "I was just being stupid," said the boy, "because I couldn't run away anyway. I've got a bad hip and I can't walk."'

The sick prisoner, lying there in his bed, was astonished that all this was known.

'Perhaps you'd rather I didn't carry on?' the driver said.

'No, please do. I like hearing about it, I like to be reminded of it. But what I can't understand ...'

'Oh, there's nothing very strange about it. There is a tramp called Georges – you may have heard of him? – who picked up the story on his wanderings and passed it on until it eventually reached the prison.'

There was a short silence after this, and then the sick man asked in a weak voice: 'What happened next with the man and the child?'

'Well, the man asked for food again. "You must have poor people coming here begging for food sometimes?" he said. "Yes, sometimes," the boy answered. "And your mother maybe gives them something?" "Yes, if she has anything in the house, she does." "Well, you see," the fugitive said, "that's what it's all about now. I'm just a poor fellow who has come begging for food. Tell me where there is something to eat and I won't eat more than I need to take the edge off my hunger!"

'The child gave him a canny look and said in an amused way: "Mother's been worrying about this escaped prisoner who is supposed to be loose in the forest. She's put all the food away and locked the larder." "You must have seen where she put the key, so you could tell me – otherwise I'll have to break in." "That won't be easy," the boy said, "we've got stout locks on our larder."

'The man searched the whole cottage for the keys, looking on the mantelpiece and in the drawer in the table, all in vain. Meanwhile the child had sat up in bed and was looking out of the window. "There are people coming up the road," he said, "Mother and a load of others." The fugitive leapt to the door in a single bound. "If you go out that way you'll run straight into them," the child said. "It would be better if you hid in the larder." The man hesitated at the door: "I haven't got a key to the larder!" "But I do," said the boy, holding out his hand and offering him a big key.

'The fugitive took the key and ran to the larder. "Throw me the key," the boy said, "and pull the door shut from inside." The man obeyed and a moment later he was locked in the larder.

'With his heart pounding, the fugitive stood listening at the larder door. He heard the door to the outer room open and people come in. Then a woman's voice shouted, loud and shrill: "Has anyone been here?" "Yes," the child answered, "a man came as soon as you'd left." "O Lord, O Heavens above!" his mother wailed. "They told me they saw him creeping out of the forest and coming this way."

'The fugitive uttered a string of silent oaths at the boy who had betrayed him. The cunning child had caught him in a rat trap. He began heaving on the door, prepared to rush out at full speed and make good his escape. Then someone asked where the fugitive had gone and he heard a clear child's voice answer: "He's not in the cottage anymore. He was scared when he saw you all coming."

'"Did he steal anything?" the boy's mother asked. "No, he only wanted food and I had none to give him." "Did he do anything to you?" "Yes, he tickled my nose with a straw," the child said, and the fugitive could hear them all laughing. "He did, did he?" the boy's mother said, and laughed with relief.

'"Well, if he's not here, there's no point in standing staring at the walls," a man's voice said, whereupon they all trooped out of the cottage. "Are you going to stay at home now, Lisa?" someone asked. "I'm not leaving Bernhard on his own again today," the boy's mother answered.

'The fugitive heard the outer door close and realised that mother and child were alone in the cottage. "What's to happen to me now," he thought. "Should I stay here or should I try to escape?" He heard footsteps approaching the larder and then the sound of the mother's voice: "You in there, don't be afraid. Come out so I can talk to you." She turned the key in the lock and opened the door. The man stepped out, shy and embarrassed. "He was the one who told me I could hide in there," he said, pointing at the child.

'The boy laughed and was so excited by the adventure that he clapped his hands in glee. "Having to lie there quietly and think his own thoughts all day is what has made him so smart," his mother said proudly, "I don't know what we're going to do with him." It was obvious to the fugitive that, because her son had taken a liking to him, she was not about to call the police. "You're right there," he said, "I only came in to get a bite to eat, but I couldn't find anything – and he wouldn't hand over the keys. He's smarter than most of the people who have full use of their legs." The woman saw right through his flattery, but was pleased to hear it anyway. "Well, we can start by giving you something to eat," she said.

'While the fugitive ate, the boy questioned him about his escape and he told him the truth from beginning to end. He had not planned to escape, but an opportunity had arisen while he was working in the prison gardens and they had opened the gates to bring in some wagon-loads of coal. The boy asked question after question, never tiring of hearing how he had managed to sneak out of town and hide in the forest. Once or twice the man said it was time for him to be going, but the boy would not hear of it, until his mother said at last: "You might as well stay here tonight and talk to Bernhard. There are so many people out looking for you that you are bound to be caught, whether you stay or whether you go."

'He was still sitting there talking to the small boy when the husband arrived home. It was dark in the room and the crofter assumed it was one of their neighbours talking to the child. "Is that you, Petter, filling Bernhard's head with stories?" he said. The boy laughed: "No it's not Petter, it's much better than that. Come and I'll tell you." His father went over to the bed and put his ear to the child's lips. "It's the escaped prisoner!" the boy whispered. "Is that right, Bernhard? I think you're just spinning a yarn." "But it's true," the child said. "He's been telling me how he slipped out of the prison gates and slept in an old log cabin in the forest for three nights. He's told me everything."

'The child's mother quickly lit a small lamp and the crofter looked at the fugitive, who had moved over to the door. "I'd better hear the whole story," the crofter said, and his wife and child, interrupting each other in their eagerness, told him. The crofter was an older man, both wise and thoughtful, and he studied the fugitive carefully as the others talked. "The poor fellow looks at the end of his tether," he thought. "Another night in that old cabin will finish him off."

'"There are plenty of tramps on the road who look more

dangerous than you and nobody suggests we should lock them up," he said when his wife and son had finished. "I'm not dangerous," the fugitive answered. "I was drunk and I lost my temper with someone who was taunting me." The crofter, not wanting more to be said while the boy was listening, stopped him from going on. "I can imagine the situation," he said.

'No one spoke for a while. The crofter sat and thought over what he had heard and the others watched him anxiously. None of them said a word to influence him. At last he turned to his wife and said: "I don't know whether it's the right thing to do, but I feel the same way as you do – if our lad has taken a liking to him, I can't throw him out." They decided that the fugitive could stay the night and leave first thing in the morning. By the following morning, however, the escaped prisoner was running such a high fever that he could not even stand up. They had no choice but to keep him with them for several weeks.'

As the driver of the death cart told the story of the fugitive's time with the crofter and his family, it was curious to see how differently the two brothers responded. The sick man lay peacefully on his bed, his sufferings forgotten and his memory dwelling on past happiness. The older brother was still distrustful, suspecting there to be some trap lurking behind it all. Time after time he tried to warn his younger brother to be on his guard, but he was unable to attract his attention.

'They couldn't risk calling a doctor,' the driver continued, 'nor did they dare go to the chemist's for medicine, so the sick man had to do without. If any visitors arrived and showed signs of coming into the croft, the housewife would stop them out in the porch and tell them that Bernhard had a rash that looked suspiciously like scarlet fever, so it wouldn't be right for anyone come near him.

'After a few weeks, when the fugitive was on the road to recovery, he thought it time to move on. It would be wrong, he felt, to continue to be a burden on these poor people. It was at this point that the family began to talk to him about something that was weighing heavy on his mind. One evening

Bernhard asked him where he would go when he left them and he answered, "Back into the forest, I suppose." The crofter's wife said: "There is nothing to be gained by going off into the wilderness. If I were you I would try to settle my business with the authorities. There can't be much joy in roaming around like a wild beast." "There's not much joy in being in prison, either," he said. "That's true, but since it has to be done, wouldn't it be better to do it sooner than later." "I didn't have much time left to serve when I escaped," he said, "but my sentence will certainly be increased now." The woman looked at him: "So escaping was a dreadful mistake, then?" "No," the fugitive answered quickly, "it was the best thing I've done in all my life."

'He looked at the boy and smiled as he said this, and the boy laughed and nodded to him. He was really fond of the child, would like to have picked him up from his bed, put him on his shoulders and taken him with him. "It will be difficult for you to meet Bernhard if you are going to be a fugitive for the rest of your days," the boy's mother said. "But it will be even worse if I let them lock me up," he answered.

'The crofter was sitting by the fire and now he joined the conversation. "We have been getting on well together," he said in his usual thoughtful way, "but we can't carry on keeping you hidden from the neighbours, especially now that you are up and about. It would be different if you'd served your time and been discharged." The fugitive suddenly became suspicious – were they trying to make him give himself up so that they would avoid problems with the police? He answered: "I'm healthy enough now. I'll be on my way tomorrow morning." "That is not what I meant," the crofter said, "but if you had been a free man, I would have asked you to stay with us and help out on the croft." The escaped prisoner was touched by this offer. He knew how hard it was for a convict to find a job, but he felt so strongly about returning to prison. He sat there and said nothing.

'The boy's condition was worse than usual that evening. "Shouldn't he be treated in hospital?" the prisoner asked. "He has been, several times, but they said that nothing will help except salt sea-bathing, and who can afford that?" "It's a long journey, I suppose?" the fugitive said. "It's not just the journey. We would also need money for food and lodgings," they answered.

'He sat there in silence again for a while, his mind wondering how he could somehow come up with the money to make a seaside trip possible. Then he turned back to the crofter and returned to the earlier topic. "It wouldn't be easy having an ex-convict working for you," he said. "Oh, that could be sorted out," the crofter said, "unless, of course, you're the kind of man who has to live in a town and can't be doing with life in the country?" "I never think about the town when I'm sitting in my cell," the fugitive said. "I think of nothing but green fields and forests."

'"When you've served your sentence, you'll be free of many of the things that trouble you so much," the crofter said. "Yes, that's what I think, too," his wife agreed.

'"Will you sing us a song, Bernhard? Or don't you feel well enough tonight? I think your friend would like it," the boy's mother said. The fugitive felt anxious, as if having a premonition of misfortune. He wanted to ask the boy not to sing, but the latter had already started and was singing in a clear and gentle voice. It was easy to forget that he too was a prisoner with a life sentence, and when he sang, all his longing for freedom and movement came out.

'Although the fugitive hid his face in his hands, the tears dripped down between his fingers. "I'll never amount to much myself," he thought, "so I must try to do something to give this boy his freedom."

'He left them the next day. No one asked where he was going, but all three of them said: "You are welcome to come again."'

'Yes, that's what they said to me,' the sick man said, interrupting the driver at last. 'Do you know, officer, that is the only beautiful thing to happen to me in the whole of my life.' He lay silent, and two tears rolled slowly down his cheeks. 'And I'm glad that you knew about it,' he continued, 'because now I

can talk to you about Bernhard … I feel as though I am free …
I feel as though I have been there with him tonight … I would
never have imagined it could be such a happy night.'

The driver leaned forward over the sick man. 'Listen to me
now,' he said. 'If I could arrange for you to go to your friends
at once – although in a different way than you have ever
contemplated – what would you think of that? If I were to offer
you the chance to escape the long years of yearning and give
you your freedom tonight, would you be willing?'

As he said these words, the driver drew his hood forward
and grasped his scythe. The sick man looked at him, his eyes
wide and slowly filling with longing.

'Do you understand what I mean?' the driver continued.
'Do you understand that I am the one who can open all prison
gates, I am the one who can lead you where no pursuers can
follow?'

'I understand what you mean,' the prisoner whispered. 'But I
would be failing Bernhard. You know that I returned to prison
so that I could serve out my sentence honourably and then be
free to help him.'

'You have already made the greatest sacrifice that was in
your power to make; as a reward for that, I can curtail your
sentence and offer you a freedom too precious to measure. You
no longer need be concerned for Bernhard.'

'But I should have taken him to the seaside,' the sick man
said. 'As we parted I whispered to him that I would return and
take him there. We ought to keep our promises to children.'

'So you won't accept the freedom I am offering?' the driver
said, rising to his feet.

'But I will, I will!' replied the sick man eagerly, taking hold of
the driver's cloak. 'Don't go. You don't know how much I long
for freedom. If only there was someone else who could help
him, but he has no one but me.'

He suddenly looked up with a little cry of joy.

'My brother David is sitting over there,' he said. 'There is no
need to worry – I can ask him to help Bernhard.'

'Your brother David!' the driver said in a voice filled with scorn. 'No, you can't ask him to protect a child. If only you knew how he had treated his own.'

The driver broke off because David Holm had come to the other side of the bed and was leaning over his brother, eager to help him.

'David,' the sick man said, 'I see before me green meadows and wide open seas. You know how long I have been locked up here, and now that I am offered freedom – true freedom – I cannot resist. But there is the child, and I made him a promise.'

'Have no fear,' David Holm said in a trembling voice, 'that boy, those people who helped you – I promise you I shall stand by them. Go! Choose freedom! Go where you will! I shall care for them. Depart in peace from your prison.'

At these words, the sick prisoner fell back on his pillows.

You spoke the words of death to him, David,' the driver said. 'Come, it is time for us to go. We are still living in darkness and slavery and it is not for us to greet a soul that has been given its freedom.'

X

'If I could only make myself heard above the awful noise of this cart, I'd say a word of thanks to Georges for the help he gave Sister Edit and my brother in their hour of crisis,' David Holm thought. 'I've no intention of doing what he wants and taking over his duties, but I'd like to show him that I recognise the support he gave them.'

No sooner had the thought crossed Holm's mind than the driver pulled on the reins and stopped the horse, as if he had been able to read what David was thinking.

'I just muddle my way through as best I can,' the driver said. 'There are times when I manage to help, but just as often I fail. Those two were easy to help across the great divide because one of them had such a longing for God's heaven and the other had so little that tied him to the earth. 'David,' the driver continued, all at once falling back into the tone of their old friendship, 'many's the time I have sat in this cart and listened, and it has occurred to me that if there was just one message I could send to people, it would be a message of certainty.'

'I can see that,' Holm said.

'You know, David, there is no sorrow for the reaper in mowing a field that is full of ripened corn. But harvesting the weak and half-grown plants is a cruel and thankless task. The master I serve considers himself above it, so he leaves all that to me, poor fellow that I am.'

'Yes, I thought that was the way of it,' Holm said.

'If people only knew,' Georges said, 'how easily I can help them cross the divide when their work is over, their duties done, their bonds almost severed, but how hard it is to free those who have brought nothing to fruition and are leaving behind all they love, then perhaps they would try to make my task less difficult.'

'What do you mean, Georges?'

'Think about this, David. As long as you have been with me, you have only heard one disease being talked about – and that's how it's been for the whole of my year. It is because that disease spreads through the unripe corn, which it is my duty to reap. When I first took charge of the death cart, I thought that if we could only wipe out that disease, my burden would become less onerous.'

'And is that the message you wanted to send back to the world?'

'No, I know better now what people are capable of. I have no doubt that their science and perseverance will eventually conquer that particular enemy. They won't rest until they are rid of it and of all the other great diseases that kill them before they are fully grown. But that is not the nub of the matter.'

'What should they do, then, to ease the driver's burden?'

'People are so eager to arrange the world to serve their own best interests that I believe the day will come when poverty and drunkenness and all the other miseries that shorten life will no longer exist. But it does not follow that the driver's task will be any less burdensome as a result.'

'What message do you want to send them, Georges?'

'It will soon be New Year's morning, David, and when people wake up the first thing they will think of is all their hopes and desires for the New Year and, indeed, for all the years to come. I would like to tell them that they should not ask to be lucky in love or to win success or wealth or power or long life or even health. I want them to put their hands together and gather all their thoughts around one prayer and one alone:

'"O God, grant that my soul may ripen before it is gathered in."'

XI

Two women were sitting deep in conversation. They had been talking for many hours, with a short break in the afternoon when they took part in a service in the Salvation Army Citadel, after which they returned to their conversation. One of the women had spent these hours trying to bring courage and comfort to the other, but she still seemed to be very far from achieving her goal.

'You know, Mrs Holm, strange as it may sound, I do believe that things are going to be better from now on,' said the woman who was offering encouragement and solace. 'I believe he has done his worst. This was something he had set himself to do in order to exact the revenge he has been threatening you with ever since you got back together. But you must see, Mrs Holm, that it is one thing to be cruel for one day and to say that the children cannot be taken away, it is quite a different thing to harbour such a murderous thought in your mind day in and day out. I don't believe that there is anyone who could live with that.'

'It's very good of you to try to comfort me,' Mrs Holm said, but it was clear that she thought that although the Salvation Army captain might not know anyone who could live with such a thought day in and day out, she most certainly did.

Captain Andersson appeared to have reached the limit of her ability to convince Holm's wife, but she decided anyway to make a fresh effort.

'There is something you should think about, Mrs Holm. I am not saying it was a great sin when you left your husband some years ago, but I do see it as an act of omission. When you left him adrift at the mercy of the wind and the waves, it did not take long for the evil consequences to become apparent. But in the last year you have tried to put things right, and you have acted as God wills us to act, which is why I believe that there will be a change for the better. The storm that was raised was a violent one and it could not be calmed so quickly, but the good work that you and Sister Edit began will bear the fruits that good works bring.'

When the captain said this, she was no longer alone with Holm's wife, for the spirits of Holm himself and Georges had entered the room while she was speaking. Holm was no longer bound hand and foot and he now followed the driver of his own free will, but when he saw where he was being led, his old anger returned. No one was dying here, so why should he be forced to revisit his wife and his home?

He was about to turn on Georges with an irate question, when Georges gave him a signal to keep quiet.

Holm's wife raised her head, as if emboldened by the other woman's firm convictions. 'If only I could believe that was true,' she said.

'It is true,' the Salvationist said, smiling at her. 'Things will change tomorrow. You will see that the New Year will bring help.'

'The New Year? Yes, I suppose it is New Year's night – I had forgotten that. What time is it, CaptainAndersson?'

'We are well into the New Year already. It's a quarter to two,' the captain answered, looking at her watch.

'You mustn't stay any longer then. You should go home and go to bed. I'm quite calm now.'

The Salvationist gave her a searching look: 'I am concerned about this calmness of yours.'

'You need have no worries about me, Captain. I know I've said some hard things tonight, but it's over now.'

'Do you think you can now put everything into God's hands and trust in Him to arrange everything for the best?'

'Yes, I can do that,' Mrs Holm said.

'I would have been quite willing to stay until the morning,

but I can see that you think it's better for me to go.'

'It's been so good to have you with me, Captain Andersson, but Holm will be home soon and it's best that I'm alone when he comes.'

After a few more words the women left the room, Mrs Holm accompanying the Salvationist to the front door to let her out.

'You heard what she said, didn't you, David?' the driver said. 'Did you notice that people actually know all that they need to know? But they do need to be given strength and support in their desire to live long and well.'

He had just said this when Mrs Holm came back in. She sat down on a chair, bent down and began to unlace her boots.

As she was sitting there, the front door banged violently and she stood up and listened.

'Is that him?' she said. 'It must be him.'

She ran across to the window and tried to see down into the dark yard. She stood there for a couple of minutes, holding her breath and peering out. When she turned back into the room, her face had altered beyond recognition; a grey pallor had spread over her skin, her lips, her eyes, as if she were covered in ash. Her movements had become jerky and fumbling and a weak tremor flickered incessantly across her lips.

'I can't take any more,' she said, standing in the middle of the room. 'I can't take any more. I must trust in God. They tell me that I must trust in God. Don't they know how I've prayed to Him, how I've called on Him? What do I have to do in order to receive His help?'

She was not weeping, but her speech came as a whimper. She was in the grip of such profound despair that she was quite clearly no longer responsible for her actions.

David Holm leaned forward and looked at her sharply. A sudden thought made him shudder as, shuffling rather than walking, she made her way across the room to the bed in the corner where the two children were sleeping.

'Oh, the pity of it!' she said, bending over them. 'They are so beautiful.'

She sat down on the floor and looked for a long time first at one and then at the other.

'I have to get away from this,' she said, 'but I can't leave them behind.' And she stroked their heads awkwardly, as if unused to doing so.

'You mustn't be angry with me for what I'm doing,' she said. 'It's not my fault.'

While she was still sitting on the floor stroking the children, the door banged again. She jumped, and then remained motionless until enough time had elapsed for her to be sure it was not her husband. Then she stood up hurriedly.

'I must hurry,' she said to the children in a strange whisper. 'It will soon be done, as long as he doesn't come and stop me.' But she still did nothing, just paced backwards and forwards across the room.

'Something tells me that I should wait until tomorrow,' she murmured, 'but what would be the point? Tomorrow will be a day like every other day. Why should he be any kinder tomorrow than he is today?'

David Holm thought of his corpse lying on the path by the church and soon to be buried in the earth as being useless for any other purpose. He wished there was some way for his wife to learn that she no longer had any need to be afraid of him.

Again there was a slight noise, this time a door opening and closing somewhere in the house. Once again the woman shuddered, and then she remembered what was in her mind. Shuffling and shambling, she moved over to the stove and began putting in wood ready to light the fire.

'It doesn't matter if he comes and finds me lighting a fire,' she said, as if in answer to some silent inner objection. 'There's no reason why I shouldn't make coffee on New Year's morning, is there, if I have to stay awake waiting for him to come home?'

David Holm felt a great sense of relief on hearing her words and he began once again to wonder about Georges' reasons for bringing him here. No one was dying and no one was ill.

The driver was standing motionless, his hood pulled far forward. He was so absorbed in his own thoughts that Holm knew there was no point in questioning him.

'He must have wanted me to see my family,' Holm thought. 'It's probably the last time I shall be near them.'

'I feel no sorrow,' he said at first, thinking there was only room in his heart for one, but then he went over to the corner where the children were sleeping. As he stood there looking at them, his thoughts went to the small boy his brother had loved so much that he had gone back to prison for his sake. He felt a deep regret that he was unable to love his children in the same way.

'I hope they have good lives, anyway,' he thought with a sudden onset of tenderness. 'They will be happy tomorrow when they hear they no longer need be afraid of me. I wonder what kind of people they will turn out to be?' He was showing more interest in them than he had ever shown before and suddenly became afraid they would turn out like him. 'I have been a deeply unhappy man,' he thought. 'I don't know why I've never taken an interest in them before. If there was any chance of returning, I'd like to come back and make sure these two turned out well.'

He stood looking at his children and ransacking his heart.

'Strange that I no longer hate her,' he muttered. 'After all she has suffered, I would like her to be happy. If there was any way of doing so, I'd like to get her furniture back and see her going to church in nice clothes on Sundays. But she will be all right now that I am out of the way. I think Georges must have brought me here to make me recognise that I should be pleased to be one of the departed.'

He gave a sudden start – his wife had uttered a weak little cry of anguish. He had been so absorbed in his own thoughts that he had not been paying any attention to what she was doing.

'The water's boiling … boiling … soon be ready … must do it now … at once … no time to lose.'

She took down a tin from the shelf by the stove and spooned some coffee into the pot. Then she took a small packet of white powder from her bosom and added it to the water.

Holm stood and stared at her, unwilling to understand what

it was she was doing.

'I'll show you, David,' she said, turning towards the room as if she could see him. 'There's enough here for the children and for me. I can't face it anymore, I can't face watching them fade away. If you just stay out for another hour or two, everything will be the way you want it to be by the time you come back.'

Holm could no longer stand and listen. He hurried over to the driver.

'For God's sake, Georges! Did you hear what she said?'

'Yes, I heard. I'm here, aren't I? I have no choice but to be present – it's my duty.'

'Don't you understand, Georges? It's not just her, it's the children too. She is intending to take them with her.'

'Yes, David, she is going to take your children with her.'

'You can't let it happen, Georges! It's not necessary now. Can't you tell her it's not necessary now?'

'I can't make her hear me. She is too far away.'

'Can't you get someone to come here, Georges? Someone who will tell her it's not necessary anymore?'

'What you are asking is impossible. I have no power over the living.'

David Holm refused to give up. He threw himself down on his knees before the driver.

'Georges, Georges, don't let it happen! Remember that you were my friend in the past. Don't let this happen to me! Don't let those innocent little children die!'

Holm looked up at Georges, begging for an answer, but Georges simply shook his head.

'I'll do everything I can for you, Georges. I refused when you ordered me to take over from you as the driver, but I will accept that task with joy if only you can save me from this. They are so small, both of them, and a moment ago I was wishing I could live in order to help them grow up. And my wife, she has gone mad tonight and doesn't know what she's doing. Have mercy on her, Georges.'

When the driver remained motionless and unmoved, Holm turned away from him.

'I am so alone, so alone,' he said. 'I don't know where to turn. I don't know whether to pray to God or to Jesus Christ. I am a newcomer in this world. Where does the power lie? Who can tell me where to turn with my prayers? Oh, poor sinful man that I am, I pray unto Thee who art Lord of Life and Death. I have no right to step forward and pray, I have broken all Thy commandments and injunctions. Condemn me to the uttermost darkness, let nothing remain of me, do what Thou wilt with me, but spare these three!'

He fell silent and listened for an answer, but the only sound was that of his wife talking to herself.

'That's it! All boiled and melted! Just let it stand to cool for a while!'

Then Georges bent down to him. His hood was pushed back and his face was smiling.

'David,' he said, 'if you mean what you said then there is perhaps a way to save them. You yourself, David, will have to show your wife that she has no reason to fear you.'

'But I cannot make her hear me, can I, Georges?'

'Not as you are now, you can't. You will have to return to the David Holm who is lying in the shrubbery by the church. Can you do that?'

Holm shuddered with terror. Human life now seemed so suffocating and deadly. Would the fresh growth of his soul cease if he returned to the earthly sphere? All his happiness was waiting for him in another world. But he did not hesitate.

'If it is possible … if I am free to … I thought I had to …'

'Yes, you're right,' Georges said, his face shining ever brighter with sublime inner beauty. 'You should be Death's driver for the coming year – unless someone else is prepared to perform those duties on your behalf.'

'Someone else?' David said hesitantly. 'Who would make such a sacrifice for a sinner like me?'

'There is someone,' said Georges. 'There is a man who has never ceased sorrowing that he led you from the paths of righteousness. He will perform your duties for you, and do so with joy since he will no longer have to grieve for you.'

Without giving Holm time to understand fully what he meant, he bent forward and gazed into his face with radiant eyes.

'David Holm, old friend, do the best you can! I will remain here until you return. You have very little time.'

'But you, Georges, what about you?'

The driver cut him short with the commanding gesture that Holm had learnt to obey. Then Georges threw back his hood and said in a loud and ringing voice:

'Prisoner, return to thy prison!'

XII

David Holm raised himself on his elbow and looked around. All the street-lights were out but the sky had cleared and there was a half-moon shining. He saw at once that he was still lying on the withered grass in the church shrubbery, in the shadow of the dark branches of the lime trees.

Without a moment's thought, he began to get up. He felt so weary, his body stiff from the cold and his head spinning, but he managed to rise from the ground. He began to stagger along the avenue, but was forced to stop and lean against a tree to prevent himself falling.

'I can't do it,' he thought. 'I can't possibly get there in time.' Not for one moment did he believe that what he had been through was other than real. His recollections of the events of the night were clear in every detail.

'Death's driver is waiting in my house,' he thought. 'I must make haste.'

He moved on from the tree he had been leaning on, took a few steps and sank to his knees, pitifully weak.

Then, at this moment of abandonment, he felt something touch his brow. He did not know whether it was a hand or lips or perhaps no more than the gentle brush of a garment, but it was enough to suffuse his whole being with blessedness.

'She has come back to me!' he rejoiced. 'She is near me once more, and she is watching over me.'

He raised his hands in ecstasy, knowing that the love of his beloved was all round him, that his love for his beloved was filling his heart with tenderness even now, even though he had returned to the earthly sphere.

In the darkness of the desolate night he heard footsteps behind him and a small figure, her head covered with a great Salvation Army bonnet, walked towards him.

'Sister Maria!' he said, as she was on the point of walking past him. 'Sister Maria, help me!'

The slum sister recognised his voice. She backed away and walked on, paying no attention to him.

'Sister Maria, I'm ill, I'm not drunk. Help me to get home.'

She found it hard to believe him but, without saying a word, she approached him, helped him stand up and supported him as he walked.

At last he was on his way home, but their progress was so slow. It could be all over by now. He stopped.

'Sister Maria, it would be a great help if you could go on in advance and tell my wife …'

'And tell your wife that you are coming home drunk as usual? She must be quite used to that!'

He bit his lip and walked on in silence, struggling to increase his pace, but his body, crippled by the cold, refused to obey.

He tried again to convince her to go on in advance.

'I have been lying there dreaming,' he said. 'I watched Sister Edit die and I saw you at her deathbed. But I have also seen my family at home and my wife has lost her mind tonight. Sister Maria, if you don't hurry there quickly, she will do something dreadful.'

His speech was weak and faltering. Taking it for granted that she was dealing with a drunk, the slum sister did not answer him. Nevertheless, she steadfastly helped him along, and he knew how great a victory over her own feelings it was since she believed him to be the cause of Sister Edit's death.

As they staggered along, a new worry came to him. How was he to make his terrified wife believe him when he could not even convince Sister Maria?

At last they came to a halt outside the gate of the yard in which he lived and the slum sister helped him open it.

'You can manage on your own now, Holm, can't you?' she said, preparing to leave him.

'Sister Maria, would you be kind enough to call for my wife to come down and help me?'

The slum sister shrugged her shoulders.

'Holm, on any other night I would perhaps have taken care of you, but I have no wish to do so tonight. Enough is enough.'

Her voice broke off in a sob and she hurried away.

As he struggled up the steep steps he was certain he was going to be too late. And how, in any case, was he to make his wife believe him?

He was close to sinking down on the steps from exhaustion and despair when he felt again a gentle touch on his brow. 'She is close by,' he thought, 'she is watching over me.' And he summoned the strength to struggle to the top step.

He opened the door to find his wife standing there in front of him, having rushed to bolt the door and prevent him entering. When she saw she was too late, she backed away towards the stove and stood with her back to it, as if there was something there she wanted to conceal and guard from him. Her face had the same rigidly fixed expression as when he had left and he knew that she had not done it yet, that he had come in time.

A quick glance at the children put his mind at rest. 'They are still asleep. I have got here in time,' he said to himself again.

He reached out his hand to where Georges had been standing a short time before and he sensed another hand taking his and clasping it.

'Thank you,' he said softly, his voice trembling and his eyes suddenly misting over.

Stumbling across the room he sank down in a chair. He could see his wife following his movements as she would have done if a wild animal was loose in the room. 'She thinks I am drunk, of course, just as Sister Maria did,' he thought.

A new wave of despair washed over him because he was so exhausted but must not allow himself to rest. There was a bed in the inner room, where he longed to stretch out and no longer have to keep going, but he did not dare go through. The moment he turned his back, his wife would still do what she intended to do. He must stay awake and keep watch.

'Sister Edit is dead,' he said with a great effort, 'and I was with her. I promised her I would be good to you and the children. You can send them to the children's home tomorrow.'

'Why are you lying?' his wife said. 'Gustavsson came her and told Captain Andersson that Sister Edit was dead. He also said that you had not gone to her.'

To his own surprise David Holm began to weep. He sank lower in the chair, oppressed by the vanity of his return to this world of laboured thoughts and unseeing eyes, robbed of his strength by the conviction that he would never be able to step outside the wall his own actions had raised around him. His yearning, his boundless yearning to be united with the soul that was hovering over him but beyond his reach opened the gates and allowed his tears to flow.

As his body shook with heavy sobs, he heard his wife's voice.

'Is he weeping?' she said to herself in surprise and disbelief. A moment later she repeated, 'Is he weeping?' She moved away from the stove and, still rather fearfully, approached him.

'David, are you weeping?' she asked.

He raised his tear-stained face to her. 'I want to become a better man,' he said, his teeth clenched almost as though he were angry. 'I want to become a good man, but no one will believe me. Is that not reason enough to weep?'

'You must know, David, how very hard it is to believe you,' she said hesitantly. 'But if you can weep, I believe you. Now I can believe you.'

And as if to prove to him that she believed him, she sat on the floor at his feet and rested her head on his knee. She sat there quietly for a while, and then she too began to sob.

He started: 'Are you weeping, too, now?'

'I cannot help it. I cannot be happy until I've wept away all the sorrows I bear within me.'

At that moment David Holm felt a gentle cool touch stroke his brow. His tears ceased and in their place his soul smiled a mysterious inner smile.

He had completed the first task laid upon him by the events of the night. It now remained for him to help the boy his brother had loved. And then to show Sister Maria and others that Sister Edit had not been wrong to give him her love. And then to raise his own home from the ruin into which it had fallen. And then to carry the driver's message to humankind. When all that was done, he would be permitted to go to the one he loved and yearned for.

David Holm sat and felt infinitely old. He had become patient and submissive, as is the way of the old. He no longer dared to hope or desire, he simply put his hands together and whispered the driver's New Year's prayer:

'O God, grant that my soul may ripen before it is gathered in.'

Translator's Afterword

Körkarlen (*The Phantom Carriage*) is both a novel of social realism, set in the slums and focusing on the evils of alcohol, family abuse and tuberculosis, and a ghost story, in which the focus is on the reforming and healing power of love. In a letter to her friend Sophie Elkan in the summer of 1912, Selma Lagerlöf wrote: 'For years now I've had in my head the plan to write a Christmas story of the kind that Dickens used to write'. A week later she returned to the same topic: 'If I could get my Christmas Carol finished and about 90 to 100 pages long I would bring it out as a little book for Christmas'. (Toijer-Nilsson 1992:382) The book was finished and sent to Bonniers in November and, with some last minute changes suggested by Sophie Elkan, *The Phantom Carriage* was published in time for Christmas. Charles Dickens's story of the spiritual reform of Scrooge after the visit of Marley's ghost was not, however, the sole stimulus to Lagerlöf's novel. In view of her fame and of her sympathy for social causes, Selma Lagerlöf was approached over a number of years by the national associations for tuberculosis awareness and for temperance to promote their aims and the setting of the story also reflects these impulses. (Karlsson xx-xxi)

*

Selma Lagerlöf's narrative triumph in *The Phantom Carriage* is to keep two balls in the air simultaneously. This is not a framework story in which the reader is moved from a primary plane of reality to a secondary plane of fantasy or transcendent reality and back; instead, the realities are entwined – entwined rather than integrated because the reader constantly remains aware of them as distinct. And nowhere is it suggested that the ghostly plane is less real than the other, that the narrative might, for instance, be read as a dream.

Lagerlöf does not rush to open the ghostly plane – the reader is first prepared for it by the 'in-between' atmosphere of the opening pages when Sister Edit is hovering between life and death and the weather itself reflects the 'betweenness'. Then comes the ghost story Holm tells the tramps in the churchyard in the second chapter. It is with the third chapter that the ghostly plane is fully introduced. This very short chapter – no more than a page in length and reminiscent in its structural position and function of the third chapter of Lagerlöf's later novel *The Löwensköld Ring* – opens with the creaking of the wheels of the death cart, a sound fortunately not audible to the living since it 'signals anguish, it signals fear – fear of all the suffering and pain man can imagine'. The chapter closes with the words that foreshadow the moral trajectory of the narrative: 'It is fortunate, then, that the sound of the creaking can be heard by one man alone, and he is a man who needs to be driven to self-contempt, distress and remorse. If that is possible.'

Notably, it is only in the third chapter that the reader is really aware of the guiding voice of a narrator in *The Phantom Carriage*. For the most part, the narrative unrolls dramatically as a series of dialogues in which the characters remember and discuss the events that have led up to the few short hours of the novel's present. The narrative device that Lagerlöf utilises in order to hold her two planes of reality simultaneously open is eavesdropping. The two ghosts, Holm and Georges, are invisible to all but those at the point of death and Georges, as Holm's spiritual guide, takes him into situations where the overheard prompts a reluctant and embittered Holm along the path to penitence. Eavesdropping, then, which we usually consider to be a plotting device – and one whose over-use often tends to make us suspect incompetent narration – is used here as a means of leading Holm to self-knowledge, penitence and reform.

*

At the heart of *The Phantom Carriage*, as so often in Selma Lagerlöf's writings, lies a message of the redemptive power of love, usually the love of women, to engender penitence and the growth of active compassion. It is this that constitutes the ripening of the soul that Georges and ultimately David Holm himself prays for on behalf of humankind. In the borderland between life and death, Holm is given a second chance to attain that spiritual maturity, partly by the example of Georges, partly by the revelation of his brother's love for a sick child, but mainly by the unswerving love of Sister Edit, a love that he at first resists and scorns but at last comes to reciprocate. But it is far from being a straightforward tale of Good defeating Evil. There are ambiguities – perceived by some critics as narrative flaws – not least in the nature of Sister Edit's love, where she learns to overcome both her human love for Holm and the blinkered self-righteous benevolence that effectively leads her to destroy Holm's family. Her journey is then over and she can say farewell. But at the end of the novel Holm's spiritual journey is clearly not over; he is on the road, but the very fact that his final prayer is 'O God, grant that my soul may ripen before it is gathered in' implies his journey is not at an end. The same implication may be drawn from his earthly perception of the celestial future he will share with Sister Edit: '… he would be permitted to go to the one he loved and yearned for.'

*

By the time Selma Lagerlöf wrote *The Phantom Carriage* she was, of course, an established and best-selling writer who had already been awarded the Nobel Prize for Literature (1909). Her international reputation was such that virtually everything she wrote appeared in translation in the major

European languages within a few years of appearing in Swedish. Although *The Phantom Carriage* was and remained one of Lagerlöf's personal favourites, the critical reception and, indeed, the public popularity of the novel were less than enthusiastic and it has tended to be given relatively sketchy and unsympathetic treatment in, for instance, literary histories ever since. (Karlsson xxiv-xxvii) Writing to her Danish translator Ida Falbe Hansen in January 1913, Selma Lagerlöf commented: 'My book hasn't had such a peaceful and pleasant reception as, for instance, *Liljecrona's Home* [her preceding book]. It has proved contentious with both the public and the critics and it hasn't gone out in anything like such a big edition. But although it does not have so many friends, those it does have seem all the warmer and we'll have to see whether *The Phantom Carriage* doesn't become a popular favourite in time. I certainly intended it to be a sermon and I don't regret that, though it's perhaps a crime against aesthetics. I say perhaps, because I'm not absolutely sure. It does seem to me that literature is the bridge over which all sorts of things can be driven into the brain: philosophy and the art of living – so why not morality and religion as well, as long as it's not made too boring.' (Toijer-Nilsson 1969:108)

*

If the novel did not achieve the popularity and acclaim Lagerlöf hoped for, the film version made by Victor Sjöström in 1920 and premiered at the Röda Kvarn cinema in Stockholm on New Year's Day 1921 certainly did. Sjöström's *Phantom Carriage*, one of a number of films he based on Lagerlöf's stories, is arguably the greatest creation of the Golden Age of Swedish silent cinema and quickly achieved international acclaim for its psychologically compelling combination of the brutally real and the ghostly – the latter created by an innovative use of double and triple exposure developed by the cinematographer Julius Jaenzon. Two later film versions of the story, one French

(*La charrette fantôme*, 1939, directed by Julien Duvivier) and one Swedish (*Körkarlen*, 1958, directed by Arne Mattsson) suffered by comparison with Sjöström's masterpiece. (Karlsson xli)

*

Körkarlen has been translated into eighteen languages. German, Danish and Finnish translations appeared in 1912, virtually simultaneously with the original (respectively, *Der Fuhrmann des Todes*, trans. Pauline Kleiber; *Køresvenden*, trans. Ida Falbe-Hansen; *Ajomies*, trans. Helmi Setälä). It is noteworthy that English and French translations (*Thy Soul Shall Bear Witness*, trans. William Frederick Harvey, 1921; *Le charretier de la mort*, trans. T. Hammar, 1922) appeared in the years immediately following the international success of Sjöström's film, as did translations into, for instance, Hungarian, Spanish and Icelandic. Selma Lagerlöf generously, if unnecessarily, gave Sjöström credit for promoting her works when she wrote to him in early 1921: 'It seems, however, that you have not only opened the road for Swedish film but also for my books...' (Sahlberg 199). The present translation was made from Selma Lagerlöf, *Skrifter: Körkarlen; Bannlyst*, Stockholm: Bonniers, 1933, in combination with the text-critical test edition with introduction and commentary by Jenny Bergenmar, Maria Karlsson and Petra Söderlund, published by Svenska Vitterhetssamfundet in 2009. I gratefully acknowledge the use I have made of the test edition both in the translation and in this Afterword.

Finally, after some hesitation and with reservations, I decided to use the title *The Phantom Carriage* rather than more literal and accurate possibilities such as 'The Driver' or 'Death's Driver' in order to echo the usual English-language title of Victor Sjöström's film.

Peter Graves
Edinburgh, March 2011

References

Karlsson, Maria: 'Inledning' in Selma Lagerlöf, *Körkarlen: Berättelse(Textkritiskprovutgåva)*. SvenskaVitterhetssamfundet, Stockholm, 2009.

Sahlberg, Gardar: 'Selma Lagerlöf och filmen' in *Lagerlöfstudier*, 1961, pp. 187-206.

Toijer-Nilsson, Ying (ed.): *Selma Lagerlöf: Brev 2*. Gleerups, Lund, 1969.

Toijer-Nilsson, Ying (ed.): *Du lär mig att bli fri. Selma Lagerlöf skriver till Sophie Elkan*. Bonniers, Stockholm, 1992.

SELMA LAGERLÖF

Lord Arne's Silver
(translated by Sarah Death)
ISBN 9781870041904
UK £9.95
(Paperback, 102 pages)

The Löwensköld Ring
(translated by Linda Schenk)
ISBN 9781870041928
UK £9.95
(Paperback, 120 pages)

Selma Lagerlöf (1858-1940) quickly established herself as a major author of novels and short stories, and her work has been translated into close to 50 languages. Most of the translations into English were made soon after the publication of the original Swedish texts and have long been out of date. 'Lagerlöf in English' provides English-language readers with high-quality new translations of a selection of the Nobel Laureate's most important texts.

VICTORIA BENEDICTSSON

Money

(translated by Sarah Death)

Victoria Benedictsson published Money, her first novel, in 1885. Set in rural southern Sweden where the author lived, it follows the fortunes of Selma Berg, a girl whose fate has much in common with that of Madame Bovary and Ibsen's Nora. The gifted young Selma is forced to give up her dreams of going to art school when her uncle persuades her to marry, at the age of sixteen, a rich older squire. Profoundly shocked by her wedding night and by the mercenary nature of the marriage transaction, she finds herself trapped in a life of idle luxury. She finds solace in her friendship with her cousin and old sparring partner Richard; but as their mutual regard threatens to blossom into passion, she draws back from committing adultery and from the force of her own sexuality. The naturalism and implicit feminism of Money place it firmly within the radical literary movement of the 1880s known as Scandinavia's Modern Breakthrough. Benedictsson became briefly a member of that movement, but her difficult personal life and her struggles to achieve success as a writer led to her suicide only three years later.

ISBN 9781870041850
UK £9.95
(Paperback, 200 pages)

Lightning Source UK Ltd.
Milton Keynes UK
UKOW051046160613

212308UK00006B/46/P